PLAYING WITH HER

Billionaire Playboys
Book 3

TORY BAKER

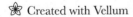 Created with Vellum

New Orleans it gave me a lot of inspiration for Amelie and Boston's story. A city that allowed me to recharge, remember that I'm more than a mom or author, and I can't be more thankful. Even if the travel hangover is real.

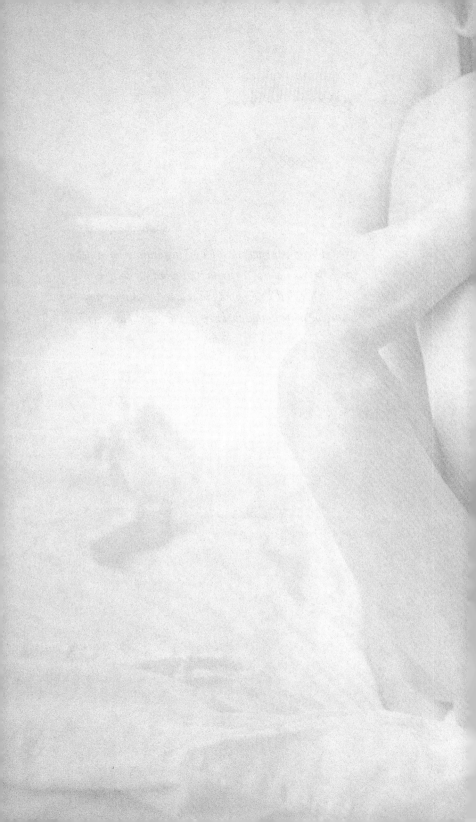

Prologue

BOSTON

One Month Earlier

CHRIST, leaving the woman beneath me in the morning is going to be fucking hard. But my brothers at Four Brothers summoned me back as an emergency, and I have no choice but to go. Pushing it off by even a day is stretching it. Parker, Ezra, and Theo may not be family by blood; they're still more than I've ever had before. What none of them know is I've fallen fast and hard. Being with Amelie is as easy as breathing.

"Fuck, I need more. Need to get deeper. Closer," I groan. Amelie's head is tipped back, her eyes are closed, and piles of her auburn hair are spread out on the mattress. The view she's giving me... Son of a bitch. Spectacular is the only way to put it—soft fair skin flush from the impending orgasm slowly trying to consume both of us. That high she was so close to achieving ebbs as I move her legs from being wrapped around my lower back. Now, one is on top of my shoulder, giving me the room I need, wanting to bottom out inside the woman who is making me feel things I've never felt before.

"Damn it, Boston. I was almost there." There's fire in her tone, rich, intense, and her green eyes with flecks of gold surrounding them pop open. She's pissed at me, and for good reason. She'll get hers soon, only this time, it'll be more intense for the both of us.

"I don't think you're too put out, are you?" I dip my body lower, my tongue sliding around her nipple, and feel the dig of her fingertips pressing into my scalp, pulling me closer. The grumble of annoyance she lets out has me suppressing a smile. Amelie wants what she wants, when she wants it. This being our last night for who knows how long, I'm going to make it last.

"Please, don't tease me." She uses her foot, planting it on the mattress, lifting her hips up to match each one of my thrusts. Each time I pull out, the ripple of her cunt has my own body locking up, all that velvet heat wrapped around my dick. I'm giving in to what she wants not because I'm a pushover. Oh no. I want the same thing she does. Amelie loves nothing more than to have my lips wrapped around her nipples, pulling the distended tip into my mouth. I swear she can come from my mouth alone and not with me between her spread legs. Nipple play alone does it for her. The way she arches her back, offering me more of her body, it's only fair that I reward us both. I suck deeply, tongue pushing her nipple to the roof to my mouth, while keeping up a steady rhythm of my hips rocking in and out of her, not as hard before, albeit deeper, hitting her cervix. I wish like hell I'd had the forethought to do away with condoms. Though, it would have me coming before her, so maybe it's a good thing after all.

"You like that, beautiful? Fuck, yeah, you do. You're taking my cock perfectly, Amelie. Christ, you're going to make me come before I'm ready." I pull away from her nipple, hand wrapping around the back of her neck, holding her, eyes locked on one another even though I won't have them for long. Amelie can't keep her eyes open while coming. We've tried. Fuck, have we ever. It doesn't matter that I'll stop mid-orgasm in order for her to open her eyes, desperately wanting her to see the rawness before she takes me with her.

"Boston!" I swivel my hips on one powerful thrust inside her. My pubic bone hits her clit. There's no way I'm going to take my hand away from the back of her neck, or from holding her leg hostage over my shoulder. My fingertips tighten against her creamy thigh, leaving a whole different impression besides wearing both of us out after this third and final round tonight.

"Come on my cock, beautiful. Squeeze the cum out of me. That's what you want, isn't it?" She nods rapidly, her wetness gliding a path. Fuck, I love how she gets off, with my fingers, my mouth, or my cock. It's a damn vision, a work of art, and it's all mine.

"Oh God, yes, yes, yes!" The tight clamp her pussy has on my cock triggers my own orgasm. I thrust my hips through hers while I reach my own, hands tingling, swallowing down the groan, and keep my eyes locked on Amelie's pretty face, her eyes slammed shut, lips pursed, high cheekbones colored with lust. I didn't move my gaze from where it's locked the entire time. There's no way I'm going to be able to move after this. Amelie's body has to be as tired as my own. It's been a marathon of sex. I told her the news yesterday, of my impending trip back home, and was unable to give her an answer of when I'd be coming back, only that I'd be here as soon as I could. A few words were threatening to come out, but it wouldn't be fair, not to her or to myself. She may not know it yet, and I'll tell her the truth one day, but I'm protecting her, leaving to put out a fire. If not for the screwup I call a father, she'd be boarding my private jet right along with me.

Amelie's limbs fall from their purchase, no longer on my body, and fuck if I don't like it. No longer is one hand at the back of my head, holding me so we're looking at one another, and the other, which was fisting the sheets beneath her, is now unclenched. I'm already missing the warmth. I allow my body to drop onto hers, giving Amelie more of my weight. My cock isn't settling down even after our third time tonight, her five orgasms to my three. Leaving her sated and sore was all a part of my master plan.

"I can hear the thoughts running through your mind. If it hasn't shut down and you're too busy thinking, that means I didn't fuck you well enough." Her arms loop around my shoulders. Glad I'm not the only one struggling here. I really should get rid of this condom, maybe catch an hour or two of shuteye before it's time for me to head to the airport.

"Tell that to my poor used and abused pussy." A laugh escapes me. Unfortunately, my cock loses her body as she joins in. Damn it all to hell. I wanted a few more minutes with her snug around me.

"She wasn't complaining a few minutes ago." Her gaze is hooded. I press my lips along her forehead. A slight sheen of sweat coats both of our bodies, and when I lick my lips, another taste of her comes right with it. "Let me take care of the condom. Be right back." She unwraps her body from mine. I watch my no longer hard cock, wetness clinging to the condom. A few things will be changing when I'm back in New Orleans and Amelie knows I'm returning.

"Alright," she responds once I'm out of the bed, situating herself beneath the covers, eyes already closing, sleep consuming her body. I head to the bathroom, keeping the light off, to take care of the condom and wash my hands, then heading back to Amelie. She's tucked into herself, hands beneath her head. Sliding in beside her would be so easy. Falling asleep with her wrapped around me would be even better. Sadly, the sun is rising all too fucking fast, meaning I've got to get my clothes on, head to the airport, and put fires out that I didn't start in the first place. The only consolation in this dynamic is I'll be coming back. I'm not playing with her. I'm playing for fucking keeps. Amelie will be in my life. Forever. Even if that means leaving now to protect her from the people who share my blood.

"See you soon, beautiful." The sun is slowly creeping up along the horizon. Neither of us took the time to close the shutters, so the orange, pink, and purple hues cast a light throughout the room. Amelie sleeps through the entire process of my redressing and kissing her lips softly, a good thing, too, because I'm not sure I could handle saying goodbye.

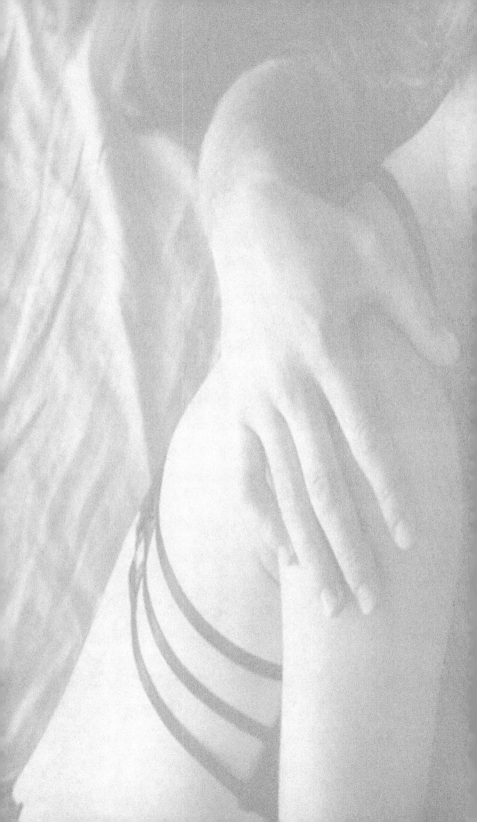

ONE

Amelie

THIS IS WHAT I GET FOR ALLOWING MYSELF TO get lost in the heat of the moment. I did what no girl or woman should do—I allowed myself to have scorching-hot sex with a man while catching every feeling there is to mankind as well. Why? He was gorgeous, gave me his full attention, his eyes spoke of an untold story, and the way he carried himself was confident in every facet you could imagine, especially in bed. I'd like to say I was using him as a distraction to get away from my parents and their incessant arguing. Obviously, it didn't work out that way. I'm thirty-four years old and still in the middle of their crap. Don't get me wrong, I love my mom; she's the peanut butter to my jelly sand-wich that holds me together. Sweet, kind, nurturing, always positive when the world is trying to steal her sunshine. My dad, on the other hand, well, yeah, that's an entirely different story. It's hard to love your father when he doesn't reciprocate or show the supposed love he claims to have for me. The problem is, I'm stuck between a rock and a hard spot, my parents' divorce, unincluded.

You see, it always comes down to meeting a man, at least that's usually how the story goes. This one isn't a New Orleans native, here on business, and is the epitome of tall, dark, and handsome. I thought it was going to be a fling, one night to let loose. Boy, was I wrong. One night turned into two, and so on and so forth. Each time he was here on business, we'd end up in bed together. There was no worrying about if my father is going to yell at my mother in that menacing tone of his, if he'll tell me I'm wasting my time and should quit working at the LeBlanc Inn, which has been in my mother's family for generations, only to work for him. Yeah, okay, no thanks. Needless to say, he can fall into one of the many holes along Bourbon Street for all I care. It's him who's the problem. Mom was never good enough in his eyes, and I'm the spitting image of my mother—our looks, the way we talk, the way we act, we're an exact mirror replica of one another. Which pisses him off further, making him loathe me entirely. I was never the boy he hoped and wished for, and I'm their only child, a product of his own issue with a low sperm count. Karma really is a bitch. Works in all the right favors, allowing Mom to really dodge a bullet in that arena.

I roll out of bed and head to the bathroom, taking care of an errand that while necessary doesn't help calm the nerves swirling in my stomach. Once I'm finished, I walk through my room in the three-story hotel, my own private quarters away from the guests on the top floor, perks of being the manager of the Inn. So, what if I have to traipse up and down the stairs several times a day? It's great exercise, plus it means even less time of having to deal with my father, who without a doubt is trying to badger Mom into giving up the Inn through the divorce proceedings she finally asked for. I'm not sure what tipped her over the edge, nor am I going to ask. I'm only glad it's finally happening. As for the Inn, well, fortunately, my great-grandparents had a stipulation in their will and how the Inn gets left behind. It went to my grandparents, and then my mother. Should something happen to her, it would go to me. Although judging by the way dear old dad is going about things and the way he attempts to manipulate the situation, it could backfire on us. I'll be rooting for my mother. No way will I allow her to go down without swinging a few punches if it means she can keep what's rightfully hers.

I take a deep breath. The piece of plastic digs in the palm of my hand, but I refuse to look down at the response as I continue my path from the bathroom. The Inn is historic in all the preservation we could afford after a long history of hurricanes, tornadoes, and everything else along the way. Hours upon hours, Mom, I, and a few other employees helped breathe life back into what my family loved as much as my mother and I have. The wood floors creak when you walk across them, sanded and refinished to a gleaming dark stain matching the trim around the whole room. The walls are painted in a muted white beige tone, there are wood tray ceilings, and plantation shutters on the door that leads to the small balcony, the windows sporting the same treatment. A plus when you're working the front desk well into the early hours of the morning, checking in out-of-towners, taking care of rooms should the guests need towels, soap, or helping them out when they're locked out after a long night out partying. I pull open the doors, ready to watch the sun rise over the water. The partial view still steadies my racing heart. No matter the complication in my life, I only hope it will do the same today. I'm still in my night clothes—an oversized shirt and sweatpants that have seen better days, hair in a bun on top of my head secured with a jaw clip. There's no coffee in my hand like usual, and my phone is charging on top of the nightstand. There's no way I could answer if my mom or best friend called. The sleep I hoped would come last night never did. Nope, instead, I tossed and turned, got up a million times praying to the period gods that mine would magically arrive. It didn't, like I was ninety-nine percent sure it wouldn't, causing me to do the one thing I wasn't prepared for even if I am well over the age of thirty. It's not like I'm married, in a committed relationship, or, you know, actually knew more about Boston than the fact he was from New York, was here on business, and the days were hot, the nights hotter, and the orgasms were fucking phenomenal. Okay, fine, I know more than that, but it's beside the point. There were no promises made. One night a month ago, he left to head back to New York. I was fast asleep, and when I woke up, there was no sign of him except a discarded handkerchief. We'll come back to that. I'm still scared to admit that I keep it in my nightstand drawer and look at it every night before I go to bed. We exchanged numbers. He didn't use mine first, so being the stubborn woman I am, I didn't use his either.

The only problem I have is how good it was between us, too good, and apparently, condoms be damned, the plastic test in my hand is cutting into my palm. I reluctantly look down. It's been well past the time the instructions said to wait. The positive line is all I need to know. I'm pregnant.

TWO

Boston

_____

"I SHOULD HAVE KEPT MY DRIVER UNTIL Boudreaux meets up with me," I tell the quiet street. Taking the company jet early this morning is wreaking havoc on my sleep schedule. My phone vibrates in my pocket. I ignore the call. I'd rather walk around the perimeter of the building one last time instead of answering my phone. Beyond the wrought-iron gate there seems to be enough space for two cars, meaning the rest of the employees will have to fight with street parking or deal with a parking garage. I'll have to figure out if a monthly allotment will be necessary for each employee or not. This new venture is my baby, a new extension of Four Brothers, which means I'll keep being on the front line, assume what needs to be done, take it back to Parker, Ezra, and Theo, and we'll agree or not then go from there.

I pull my phone out of my pocket and dial my driver, ignoring the missed calls from my father, mother, and Parker. It's too fucking early, and I don't have enough caffeine in my body. Noticing the time, I grimace because I've rearranged my schedule only for Boudreaux to be a damn no-show. If I lose this damn place, I'm going to be pissed as hell, and while I may not be well-known in this area of the world, that doesn't mean I'll let shit lay where it lands. Being told this deal was locked and loaded only for it not to be means heads are going to fucking roll.

"Mr. Wescott, how may I help you?" Scott, the hired driver I acquired while I was down here the last time asks. Using him again was a no-brainer. Him answering on the first ring solidifies that I chose the right company. At least one thing is going right today.

"Can you please pick me up at the location you dropped me off? From there we'll be going to LeBlanc Inn," I tell Scott.

"Of course. I'll be there in less than five minutes." I hang up, thumb through my texts until I get to our group chat.

> Me: The purchase may fall through; I'll catch you up as soon as I make it to the Inn.

Since Parker called only minutes ago, it's no surprise he's the first one to respond.

> Parker: Fucking sucks. You
> need Sly?

> Theo: The fuck? You're suddenly
> ready to up and move to New
> Orleans and can't close a deal?

I laugh. This motherfucker is lucky he's like a brother to me. The house I've purchased is currently being rented back to the owners until the end of next week, and this deal, well, it should have been closed by the end of this week.

> Me: Your mom wasn't saying that
> last night.

> Theo: Eat a bag of dicks.

> Ezra: The fuck? It's too damn
> early for this shit. Call if you need
> something. It's the least I can do.

> Parker: I'm out. Call later.

> Me: Give me a couple of hours.
> We'll do a conference call.

I pocket my phone when I hear footsteps approach and figure it's Boudreaux, but when I look up, it's the last person I expected to see— the woman I left in her bed last month, soft, sweet, and sated. That's not the case now. Nope, she's walking toward me with fire in her eyes, and it's zeroed in on me.

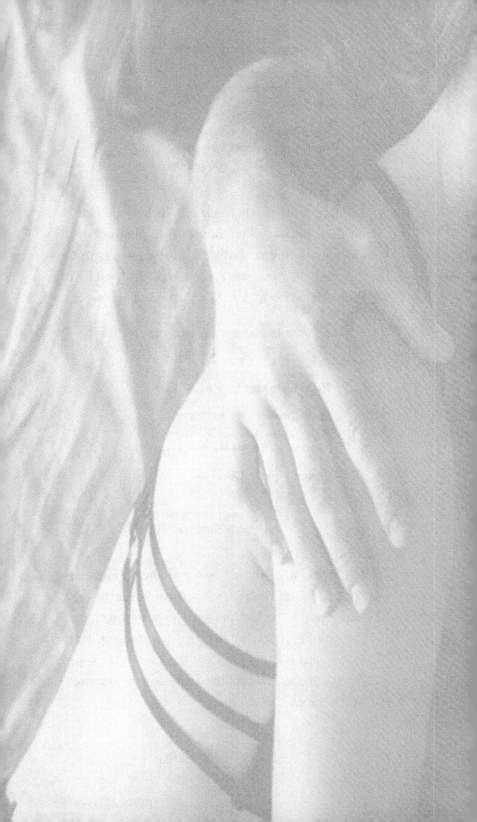

THREE

Amelie

AFTER THE SHOCK OF MY LIFE, I GOT MY SHIT together. Nothing like needing to pull your big girl panties up, get dressed, put on makeup to hide the inner turmoil that hovers on the edge of a hot pot of water ready to boil over, only it's inside of you. Sadly, this time, it's not from partying with my best friend, Eden. The hurricanes we consumed months and months ago are not threatening to come up. Oh no, it's having to explain to my mom and eventually Boston that there's a proverbial bun in my oven. I was in for the second shock of my life when I walked downstairs to the argument of all arguments, so loud that I'm sure our guests could hear it, but I wasn't about to break it apart. My mother was losing her shit, rightfully so. My great grandparents owned more than LeBlanc Inn. We own another building, this one along the riverfront, sitting empty for the time being. Since there's a divorce in the works, my mother's attorney suggested to leave it alone because starting another venture capital would be stupid and might open her up to a fine-tooth comb to be raked across the coals, you know, like paying him more money when he has plenty of his own.

"How could you!" I yell as I walk up to Boston, for so many reasons I can't even begin to get them all out. Never in all my years did I think I'd come face to face with the father of my child, who's turning out to be a snake in the grass. How I'm able to compose myself is beyond me. I'm the type of person who when I get mad, I become emotional. Tears do not threaten to come; they roll down my cheeks without my permission. I'm not a baddie with an attie, meaning my bad-ass persona is not there, and neither is my attitude. Sure, I've got the red hair to prove I've got a temper, but other than that, I'm a pile of waterworks when I'm riled up. My father should be selling his own building. He owns it free and clear but didn't take care of it through the years, leaving it riddled in shambles, so it's less habitable than the one Boston currently standing in front of, which means it's less profitable. If you guessed my father was a greedy money sucker, you'd be right.

"How could you!" I shout again when I'm closer, my voice carrying along the street, the water only echoing it more. I'm about over today and all these unwanted emotions swirling inside of me. The father of my child, who impregnated me unknowingly, or did he? No way. He couldn't be capable of stealthing me, right? Why would he purposely poke holes through a condom? You only hear about that stuff on social media, at least that's where I've heard it. The plethora of questions are now making me second-guess every single thing. I mean, if he's so willing to purchase a piece of property from my father, then I suppose there's a possibility he'd be capable of anything.

"Hello to you, too, Amelie," Boston responds, standing there with his hands in his pockets, looking like the perfect gentleman in what I'm sure is his five-thousand-dollar suit, his dark hair clipped short on the sides as well as the top. The beard along his jaw has my thighs clenching, which is no easy feat when I'm steadily marching toward him, ready to smack the smugness off his handsome face. His obsidian-blue eyes twinkle, making me recall the last time we slept together, not that much sleeping actually happened. Boston was leaving, unsure of the next time he'd be back down here, but he was adamant he'd be back. I began to lose faith after two weeks. We had a marathon of sex, him powering into me from behind, hand wrapped around my throat, the other gripping my hip so tightly I was left with marks the next day. That was only the first round. The second time was just as hurried and frenzied, me riding him, his fingers working my nipples, my thighs aching so badly I was tempted to ask him to take over, but there was no way I could have or would have. Instead, I rode him hard, bouncing on Boston's thick cock. No wonder I'm pregnant. The man is impressive in the length department. I swear he hit my cervix a few times. The third time is one that will last in my memory for a lifetime. We held each other's eyes for the majority of the time, and it seemed he needed to be as close as possible, sitting inside me well after we orgasmed together. I stomp out the memories. I'm too upset for more than one reason.

"Don't you 'Hello Amelie' me. I know what you're doing here. How could you get Amelie Boudreaux in bed, mess with her head, then go straight to my asshole father?" I get closer, my pointer finger hitting him right in the chest as I lay into him. My radar on picking a good man is obviously off, unlike Eden, who is now completely and totally head over heels in love with her judge. Sadly, it doesn't look like the man in front of me will ever be that for me. It's not like he gave me the slightest clue that he was Mister Forever, more like Mister Right Now.

"What the fuck are you talking about?" I take a step back at his question and see the flare of anger in his eyes. Me backing up is what's making him upset, unlike me raising my voice.

"What do you mean, what am I talking about? Boston, who can't so much as use a phone to text and say hey, I'm going to buy your mother's building from underneath her, that's what I'm talking about!" Shit, I did not want to show my cards. A poker player I am not. I could have used the phone as well. Him leaving without so much as a goodbye made me lock my cell each time I hovered my thumb over his name.

"You're going to have to clue me in, Amelie. I've got no damn idea what you're talking about." He closes in on me, is moving closer. I have to take two steps for every one of his. The only scents around us are that of the river and the unique scent of the domineering man in front of me. My back meets the brick wall of my great-grandparents' building. The heat coming from both the building and Boston does little to calm my rapidly beating heart.

"My father, the asshole you're supposed to meet to buy this building. Ring any bells? It's not like there are a lot of people with the last name Boudreaux running around in New Orleans." My father is the last in the line to carry the family name. Good freaking riddance. If there were a picture under the term *narcissist* in the dictionary, you'd find Noah Boudreaux the Third. The man will tear you down, not with his fists; that would mean he'd have blood on his hands, and he would never. Dear old dad likes to use his words, ruining your confidence with one biting sentence at a time.

"Amelie." My name coming from his lips is harsh, unlike the times he'd say it when he was buried deep inside me, a long guttural groan. "Still not ringing any bells, beautiful. The last time I came down here, this place was listed for sale through an MLS, not some damn website. I emailed the listing agent, clearly having no idea you were tied to it in any way. I've got no clue what you're trying to pin on me. I'd suggest you take a breath, gather your shit, and come at me with a clear fucking head." This is where I'm going to blame my pregnancy hormones. Who cares if I only found out about the impending baby an hour or so ago? When Boston's voice comes out deep and demanding, my body has no damn control over itself. Adding to the display of manliness is the way I'm caged in. His forearms are braced on the brickwork on either side of my head, and the knee he has wedged between my now spread thighs only enhances my desire for him. Even if my mind is shouting at me to run away, my traitorous body is melting for him.

"Boston." I try again, this time running every-thing through my head, dissecting what he's just told me. My head tilts back, the thud harder than I would have liked. Clearly, Boston isn't a fan of it either because he mutters, "Christ, Amelie, no need to cause brain damage." I ignore him, though, and close my eyes, taking a deep breath, once again listening to Boston's voice of reason. I shouldn't feel this hit to my chest. My heart shouldn't ache. This is who Noah Boudreaux is, yet it still surprises me.

"Boston, this property isn't for sale. It belongs to my mother. I'm not sure what my father thought he could get away with or how he could swindle his way by selling this out from underneath a family estate, but that's who he is." I refuse to apologize for the rage I sicced on him. It was warranted, even if I might have been in the wrong a teeny tiny bit.

"Yeah, well, I'm figuring that out. If I let you go, are you going to knee me in the balls? I'd like to have kids one day." That sobers me up quickly. I'm still unsure how or when I'm going to tell Boston that I'm pregnant with his child. I only know that this isn't a secret I'll keep from him, at least not for long.

FOUR

Boston

"WE'RE GOING TO CIRCLE BACK TO THAT. Now, you don't know me, at least who I truly am. You want to get to the heart of me, I'm all for that. New Orleans is my permanent residence as of next week. The building I was hoping to lock down was for the company my brothers and I own together. The bomb I'm about to drop on you will tell you I'm not the scum beneath your shoe, lumping me in with the asshole you call your father. I've got one of my own, Amelie. I'm Boston Westcott, son to the biggest dick in New York, if not the entirety of New England. What I am is not him." I take a deep breath and wedge myself further between her spread thighs. The way she had no problem giving me the in I needed with one knee, and feeling the way she settles around me, pelvis to pelvis, I'd say she still wants me, weeks later without me so much as sending a text or a phone call. There was a

27

reason behind that, and it wasn't the media attention. Much like Amelie's father, an asshole in his own way, Governor Wescott would hang her out to dry, reveal her deepest, darkest secret, exposing her until there's nothing left but the shell of the woman, all in order to reel my ass into his three-ring circus of political bullshit.

"Oh fuck," she sighs as my cock notches along the heart of her, scaring me with her heat. Her white linen shorts would be so easy to divest her of. One pull of the strings, a shimmy of her hips, and she'd be bare. It's a temptation. Too bad my consciousness is tugging at me to step away, to lose the sweet woman I'm pressed against, for the time being.

"Yeah, beautiful. It seems we've got more to talk about. Maybe against your great-grandparents' building isn't the right place, and out here in the open isn't the right time." I move, hands leaving the warm brick and going to Amelie's hips, gripping them like I have many times before. The edge of her shirt lifts up, giving me the smooth skin of her mid drift. Unable to resist the lure, my thumbs sweep across the light tone against my darker. Damn, my cock is aching to get back inside Amelie's tight little body.

"Is it even a good idea for you to be seen with me?" Her statement breaks the haze of lust, pissing me off. Clearly, Amelie Boudreaux knows all about the Wescott family. It'd be hard not to.

Dad's next move is heading for Presidency, and I want fuck all to do with the shit that comes along with it. There's a reason the escape from New York came at the time it did. That's also why my father can't stop blowing up my phone, causing me to block his number, along with his minions' each time an unknown number appears.

"We'll be talking about that, too. Don't like the way you're thinking about yourself. That's a reflection of my shit touching you." I should have made an effort to call or text her. "Now, let's go. We'll head back to LeBlanc Inn, I'll check in for the week, and we'll talk without having to worry about others overhearing." I pull her away from the brick, hearing a car idling over my shoulder. My hand takes hers, and I lead her toward the car.

"Boston, I can walk to the LeBlanc. It's only a few streets away." Amelie puts the brakes on our walk.

"Why, when we're both going in the same direction?" I ask. Finally, she allows me to guide her to the back door, reluctantly. I open it, and Amelie slides inside. I follow her. Scott doesn't say a word, only nodding his head. The door is barely closed behind us when he's heading to LeBlanc Inn. The driving down here in New Orleans is similar to New York City, though I'm not sure our potholes are quite this bad. It works in my favor, though, especially when Scott has to take a sharp turn to avoid colliding with another car on the narrow streets. Amelie is pressed against me, board straight, and I've got one fuck of a feeling that we have a lot of shit to talk about. This purchasing the building is only the tip of the iceberg.

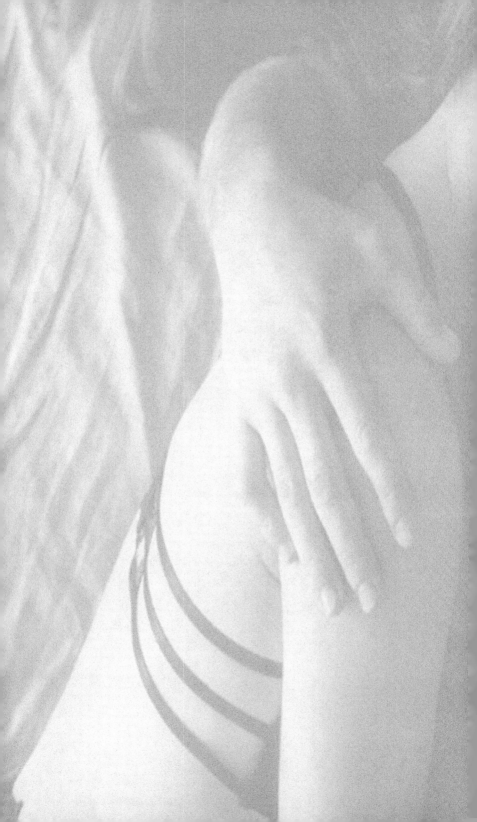

FIVE

Amelie

"AT LEAST HE'S GONE, FOR NOW," I TELL THE window. He'll be back. He always is, especially since Mom moved out of their once shared home, not taking anything except her personal items. We turn into the small parking lot. I'm back in my designated seat, no longer pressed against Boston even though he felt good and smelt just as delicious as before.

"Did you say something?" Boston asks. I shake my head, not needing to repeat anything since it was inconsequential anyway. I'm opening the door the very second Scott, Boston's driver, puts the car in *Park*. The automatic locks give way, and I'm out, taking a deep breath. *Overwhelmed* is the only word I can use for what is going on my head.

"Come on, we need to talk to Mom, and fast, then probably her attorney. I hate to bring you into my family drama. The divorce has been nasty, and it's only getting nastier by the hour. She needs as much documented evidence as she can get." This is the least he can do for me, also while I'm walking at a steady pace toward the side entrance, away from where the guests usually mingle.

"Amelie." Boston's hand wraps around my wrist, stopping me from taking the first step up the small concrete stoop where, when I was a girl, I'd eat the cookies Mom would bake for new guests. She'd save a few for me for when I came home from school as an afternoon snack. "Give me a second. If you're going to need a statement from me, the least you can do is look at me. Damn, not ten minutes ago, there was nothing between the two of us. What's with the wall, beautiful?" Boston has no idea. This is the real me when we're not shrouded in darkness. My guard is always up; my father made sure of it.

"Much like I don't know you, you don't know me. This version is the one I have to keep up, especially when there's a chance my father will return." That's partially the truth. The other flip of the coin is, well, I've got a secret of my own, one that I really need to talk to Eden about first, figure out where to go from here before I finally tell Boston.

"Fair enough. I'll give your Mom's attorney a statement. I'll need to have mine on the phone through the process." Crap, this is becoming a fiascos neither of us deserve to get involved in, least of all Boston.

"Shit, I didn't even ask with your name and all. Is it even a smart idea to do this?" My shoulders droop, ass dropping to the step. Boston's hand around my wrist disappears. A tiredness like no other hits me deep in my bones, the lack of sleep, dealing with my father, Boston showing up, not to mention the elephant looming above us.

"Considering I'm not my father, yes. It'll be fine. I'm still going to make sure everything is done well above board. Too many variables can result from this. Are you okay?" Boston asks, sitting down beside me. His arm wraps around my back, pulling me closer to his intoxicating scent. I shouldn't be this close to him, allowing my walls to drop and about to tell him more of my life than anyone would ever want to know.

"Yes, no, maybe. I'd kind of like to rewind time, go back to yesterday, sleep without tossing and turning, thinking about the what-ifs, sleep in, not come downstairs hearing my father in a rage, worried he was going to esca-late." My father has yet to raise his hand to my mother. I fear it's only a matter of time, though. One wrong move, and he'd do what-ever he could to make her give him what he wants. Money, power, greed—that's who he is, worse now since Mom is finally filing for divorce.

"I have a lot of money, Amelie, but I'm pretty sure it takes more than cash to turn back time. Hell, you'd probably need some scientist, and even then, it wouldn't matter. If it wasn't what they want, not even my billions can make it happen." My head pops off his shoulder. Why I let myself do that is beyond me.

"I'm sorry, did you just say billions? Holy fuck, I really don't know you, not at all." My family is not rich. We don't have a politician's name attached to ours. What we do have is a family name that's been passed down from generation through generation. We're well known around this area. Humble is how I'd categorize us. We're not rolling in the dough, and when we do have extras of anything, it's donated. Food especially. Any money we do have is attached to buildings, the hospitality industry, and all that.

"We've got a lot to talk about. Part of that is my permanent residence down here. Sorry about your luck, but you aren't getting rid of me that easily, Amelie." He bumps our shoulders together.

"I'll say." Another worry pops up out of me from nowhere. Boston having as much money as he says he does could make my life pretty unbearable. Just what I need, another freaking concern.

"No kidding. Please excuse me while I pick my jaw up off the ground." I say. Jesus, all the doubts keep piling up, one on top of the freaking other.

"Oh, sorry, I didn't mean to interrupt. I'll, umm…yeah, go back inside." We break apart as if we're two teenagers getting caught sucking face.

"It's okay, Mom. Mom, as you know, this is Boston Wescott. Boston, this is my mom, Isabelle. Everyone calls her Isa, though," I formally introduce the two. We stand up in unison. I wipe the back of my shorts off. Dumb move on my part, sitting on concrete with white bottoms.

"It's nice to meet you. I can see where your daughter gets her beauty from," he turns on the charm, and my mother is silently eating it up.

"Nice to meet you as well. Won't you come in? I'm pulling a breakfast casserole out of the oven now." The Southern Belle comes easily with my mom, mainly because that's who she is through and through.

"Yes, we will. Boston is going to tell you what happened and what Daddy has been doing behind your back. He's also staying for the next week or so. Obviously, you've seen the books. If we can make a room available for him, I know he'd be happy, and really, he's about to do us a

massive favor." Mom looks me over carefully.
She of all people knows what her future ex-
husband is capable of doing.

"We can do something for that, not that he'll
actually be in his room at night." My mother
and her verbal vomit states. Boston's eyes lock
on mine. There's no way my face isn't showing
exactly what I'm thinking. This day, I'm going to
need coffee, and a lot of it. Stat.

"Okay, this has been a fun conversation," I
groan, unsure if I should laugh or cry. Instead, I
go with, "Mother, if you'll lead the way," shut-
ting down any further discussion about Boston
and me, using my hand in a fluttering movement to shoo her inside the door. My other goes
to Boston. No need to have employees gossiping
more than they have already.

"Wow," Boston mouths once Mom gives us her
back. I close my eyes and take a deep breath,
muttering, "Yep, that's my mother," under my
breath. The sooner this is over, the sooner I can
talk to Boston, alone and in my room.

SIX

Boston

"THE LAST TIME I WAS DOWN HERE, MY REALTOR showed me what I know now is your building; an MLS was online beforehand. There was no screwing around with that. You may want to let your attorney know now, it was still up as of this morning when I was on the plane," I finish telling Isa the chain of events from last month to today between taking bites of her breakfast casserole made of eggs, sausage, cheese, and some kind of bread. She offered hot sauce, a Louisiana staple with most meals, but there's no way I can handle a meal too spicy in the morning unless it's a Bloody Mary. Since that wasn't offered, I went with coffee, black and steaming, so hot it nearly burned my damn tongue when I took the first sip.

"I'll get on the phone with him now. Are you sure writing a statement won't take up too much of your time?" Isa asks over the cup of her coffee. She's got the same auburn hair as Amelie, only hers is shorter and reaches her shoulders.

"Nope, I'd prefer a written affidavit. I'll have my lawyer contact your lawyer, then they can go from there." I take another bite of my breakfast, eyes locking on Amelie, who's been unusually quiet since we sat down.

"Are you not hungry, honey?" My eyes go from Isa's to Amelie's and notice that her coloring has gone from a slight flush to a white paler version of her normally fair complexion.

"Not really. Actually, I think I'm going to go lie down. I'm really not feeling that great." She stands up hastily, causing the chair to screech across the white-and-black checkered flooring. I'm out of my own when I notice her eyes closing, body swaying, and barely make it to her as Isa and I watch her body give out.

"Oh my god, oh my god!" Isa scurries around. My hands are full, trying not to jostle her, one arm going beneath the fold of her legs, the other beneath her neck.

"Isa, calm down, take a few deep breaths." I notice she's pacing back and forth, a hand covering her mouth, completely out of it, worried yet having no idea what to do.

"You're right. Shit, shit, shit." Gone is the prim and proper woman. In her place is a woman who's worried about her daughter. "Okay, I'm better now. Alright, let's get her upstairs. Can you carry her? It's three flights, and, well, I know she wouldn't want to be under the scrutiny of other people's prying eyes."

"I can carry her. Lead the way, please." I'm already going through a list of contacts to call. Parker would work. Hopefully, Nessa isn't at work. She can walk me through a list of what to look for, potential issues, and if I should call an ambulance. My other option is to call for an ambulance. It's overkill, I'm well fucking aware. I'm kicking my own ass, worrying myself too much thinking about if this could be something worse than a lack of eating breakfast, the stress from her parents' argument, and then the argument in which she blew up on me.

"I'd offer my bedroom, but Amelie would get up the second her eyes popped open, take the stairs, we'd both grumble, and it would get us nowhere." Isa guides us to a small staircase off the kitchen away from the one out front. Thank fuck. No one needs to know that Amelie is conked out in my arms. Much like me, she's a private person. I am because of the wealth and political background I come with, some people thinking they can take advantage or use me as an in with my father. It happened once, and I saw it from a mile away after what happened to

Parker, turning him into a recluse in many aspects. It wasn't what I wanted, so I kept to myself, thoroughly vetting anyone I dated. My brothers gave me hell for it. One time, that's all it took for me to break down the reasoning. All three of them sat stoically after I gave them a few words of wisdom. Parker and Ezra faired fairly well with their wives, leaving me and Theo as the confirmed bachelors of our group.

"Two more flights of stairs. Why my daughter wouldn't take the first-floor room across from me, I'll never know. She insisted on using the third floor, probably to keep me out of her business. Fat lot of good that did her. As if a mother's intuition is ever wrong. You two weren't as stealthy as you thought." We make our way up the staircase without me saying a word. Amelie's weight is slight, but that's not what has me quiet. It's how to reply to her mom. My own isn't this outspoken, a true testament to being a governor's wife, much like their children. My father prefers us to be seen and not heard. A task that's hard to follow when you break from the mold and use your trust fund to help three college buddies make something out of nothing in a run-down apartment. When we made it big, the first thing we all did was buy a place with the money each of us earned.

"Finally," Isa mutters. She takes a set of keys out of her apron pocket, slides Amelie's into the lock, and spins it around in a full circle. I hear the clicking of the tumble, and the door is open. The LeBlanc Inn is historic, lovingly restored, keeping as much of the preservation as possible, including using room keys instead of keypads or a card to slide into a slot.

I place Amelie on the bed. Her eyes flicker beneath her closed lids, and I hope it won't be long until I can see her pretty green eyes. "Can you make a cold compress? I'm going to take off her shoes. Maybe she'll come to soon," I say. My gaze travels down the length of her body, looking to see if maybe an article of clothing or a piece of jewelry is too tight, causing her to faint.

"Of course." Not seeing anything out of place, I deftly untie one shoe, then the other, tossing the white canvas sneakers to the floor. Isa returns quicker than expected.

"Mom, Boston, what are the two of you doing in my room?" Amelie opens one eye at a time, squinting as Isabelle lays the cold washcloth along her forehead.

"You fainted. Boston carried you up the stairs. Are you feeling any better, honey?"

"I'm fine." She attempts to sit up, but her body protests. I'm move closer and set my hands on her shoulders, firmly yet gently pressing them down until she silently listens.

"You're not fine. I'm calling Nessa, and if she doesn't give me the right answer, I'll either take you to the doctor or have one come here." Amelie rolls her eyes.

"I like him, Am. I'm going to go take care of a few things. You're off the clock for the entire day. I don't want you leaving this room unless Boston says it's okay, you hear? Even then, I'll bring you up food and hot tea."

"I'm not going anywhere, promise. But no food. Don't talk about it, don't bring it around, please, I'm begging you." I arch an eyebrow, wondering if maybe she has the stomach bug. No fucking way could the two of us end up like Parker and Nessa, both of them getting sick, one after another; it also helped them get where they are today.

"Fine, but I'm bringing hot tea and toast. Final answer." Amelie nods. Isabelle swoops down, pushing a few tendrils of hair off her forehead and placing a kiss there before heading for the door.

"Amelie."

"I have something I need to tell you," we say at the same time. My hackles are rising. My phone is already out of my pocket, thumb hovering over Nessa's contact, when her hand covers mine. A tightness in my gut makes me stop, waiting for her to continue.

SEVEN

Amelie

"I'M PREGNANT." GOD, I'M AN IDIOT, BLURTING out the reason why I was suddenly ready to blow chunks at the smell of cooked eggs. An aversion to food is what this baby has given me so far, along with sore boobs, which are so sore even a bra hurts. *Yay me*, I grumble internally. So, I missed a period, an overwhelming sickness to my mother's cooking of breakfast, and boobs that are trying to make me cry at the merest touch.

"How far along?" Boston, who is always composed, is losing his shit. His hand is running through his hair, and he is pacing the side of the bed. I get it. Where he is right now I was hours ago. It's a lot to take in. Though, my intuition was blinking like a yellow light at an intersection warning about caution ahead, the street is curving, and that curve is going to be your belly before too long. After he's done pacing between the foot of the bed and the nightstand, he finally stops and sits down next to my hip, hands pulling my shirt up, confusing me.

"I'm not exactly sure. What are you doing?" I ask when Boston has my abdomen completely bared then attempts to pull down my shorts. "Umm, Boston, I know this is a lot to take in, but sex isn't the way to talk through our problems." He doesn't say anything, instead murmurs a few words. Too bad they're too low to decipher. Instead, another bout of nausea hits me. Getting up is going to be a hardship, especially with the way Boston is currently cradling my stomach. No words leave his mouth. Our combined breathing is the only noise in the room.

"Give me a moment. Shit, I've got to call Nessa." My eyes bulge, at him bringing another woman into this. I reach for a pillow beside me and hit him upside the head with it while he's unaware. "Jesus, what was that for?"

"I tell you I'm pregnant, and all you have to say is another women's name. Gee, I don't fucking know why I'm ready to suffocate you at this very moment. Please move. I've got to use the bathroom." Boston takes the down-filled weapon away from me, annoying me further as he's taking his sweet time to give me an explanation. And judging by the riot that's rolling inside me, chest burning, I really won't have enough time to hear his excuse. "Gotta go. Move." I move my legs, hand going over my mouth, the sensation almost too much to bear.

"I've got you." Boston swoops me up in his arms yet again. God, I really hope none of the guests or employees have seen more than they need to today. He's fast, using his shoulder to press the switch to the on position. Artificial light blares down on us, and I catch a glimpse of Boston and myself in the mirror. He looks no worse for the wear, while I'm the one who looks ten shades of white, with dark circles beneath my eyes.

"This is not how I imagined telling you or how my day would go. You can let me down. Close the door on your way out." My feet hit the cold tile floor, and I realize yet again that Boston has completely taken care of me. Socks are the only thing on my feet.

"I'll be staying here." The retort lodges in my throat. I flip up the lid to the toilet, gather the loose tresses of my hair, and toss it to the side in a makeshift ponytail right when my stomach revolts. The noise is disgusting, and the only thing I can think about is how I didn't even drink to get this way. There was no walking down Bourbon Street, day drinking with my best friend to deserve this shitty feeling. Nope, it's Boston's child inside me saying, "Hey, Mom, eating for the foreseeable future is off the table."

Gee, thanks. This is a party favor I would have liked to politely said no thank you to.

"Christ, Amelie. Nessa is a nurse. You've fainted, now you're dry heaving. I'm either calling my best friend's wife or an ambulance. Your choice." I hear the water running. My head is resting on my arm while I attempt to regain a semblance of my bearings. Pretty sure I'm zero for zero on that today.

"I'm better. Eggs. The smell. It triggers nausea. Luckily, I hadn't eaten yet this morning, or it would have been really bad. You're not calling an ambulance. Women have been knocked up for centuries upon centuries. None of them had some crazy alpha-possessive man carting them off to the hospital with a pregnancy diagnosis." Boston hands me another wet washcloth. I wipe it down my face and neck, wiping away the sweat from my body purging absolutely nothing.

"Fine. You pass out again, your ass is going to the hospital. I barely fucking got to you. Jesus, you took years off my life, Amelie." His hand goes out to mine. I take it, still wobbly on the inside. I'm sure attempting to do this on my own would result in another grumble and him carrying me.

"To be fair, I wasn't trying to pass out. Lack of food, stress, morning sickness, finding out I was pregnant this morning. I'm still trying to figure that out. We used condoms, for goodness sake. I get they're not one hundred percent fail proof, and don't give me that look, that thought crossed my mind for two seconds before it evaporated into thin air." Boston has no reason to poke holes into a condom or try to cover up the fact if a condom broke. Plus, I'd feel it if he came inside me. There would have been a big mess we'd both had to deal with afterwards.

"Fuck, I can't believe you're pregnant with my child." His arms wrap around me and pull me closer. My hands are tucked into my chest, fingers digging into his chest, head tipping back to look into his blue eyes I've missed so much.

"Yeah, me either. I really am okay, Boston."

"I'm not one hundred percent sure how to navigate this. I know this is your body and you get the option. Fuck, I really hope we're on the same page." At the slightest suspicion of pregnancy, I was already planning, uncaring if Boston was in my life or not. My baby would be loved and cherished.

"Boston, I hope we are, too, and if we're not, that would suck. I'd never make you be a part of something you didn't want to be around for, that being my baby." A look of relief crosses his face. I keep going, "There was never any doubt in my mind I'd be doing anything but keeping the life we created."

"Yeah, good, I'm glad." The infallible Boston Wescott is nervous—the swallow of his emotions, a glossiness coating his eyes… Yep, I'd say we're totally on the same playing field. "I'm still calling Nessa. She knows about this shit. We need to get you to a doctor, keep you off your feet." I arch both of my eyebrows, ready to roll my eyes at him next. "Find you some food that will keep you from running to the bathroom." While the last part of his statement is sweet, my stomach is rolling once again. One thing is true: at least I was smart enough to schedule an appointment once two lines showed on the pregnancy stick. After that, I'll tell my mom as well as Eden. I can hear the screaming from both of them, happiness, excitement, a cause for celebration. Neither of them would cast any kind of judgment. Single, married, my mom would be over the moon to have a grandchild. She was probably worried I'd never give her one, and with me being the only child, it fell on me to potentially hand Mom over what is a pot of gold in any true parent's eyes.

"Oh God, can we not use the *f*-word right now? My stomach is not happy. This child of yours is going to give me a run for my money." Boston's smirk has a different effect on my stomach. The nausea subsides, and in its place is a completely different sensation, one I'm going to blame on pregnancy hormones. I mean, why not?

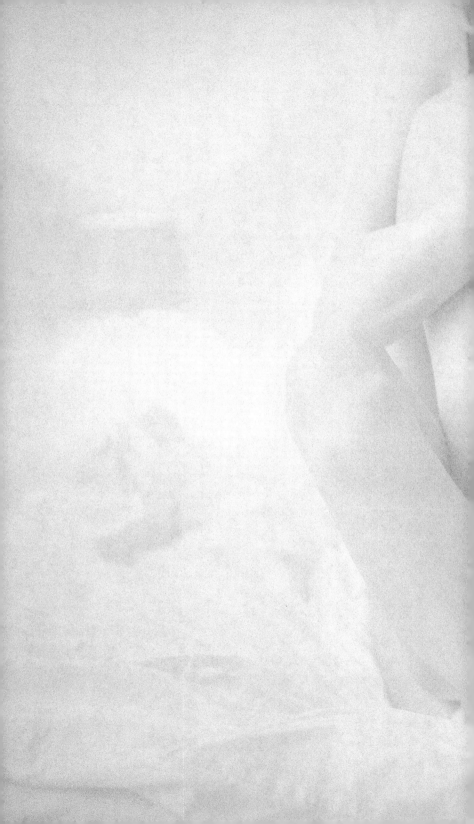

EIGHT

Boston
___

AMELIE GIVES ME MORE OF HER WEIGHT, HEAD tipping up a little bit more. I close the distance. Fuck, didn't think this is where I'd be at this point in time. Can't say I'm upset about it either. Our lips barely touch when I hear a noise. Isa will be here in no time; the heavy thuds of her feet along the staircase give us a forewarning. "No wonder you went board stiff when I talked about my boys and wanting kids. Seems my boys are already working in my favor." Amelie doesn't get a chance to reply with a witty comeback. I'm saved by her mom.

"Yoo-hoo, tea and toast at your service." Her voice is chipper and cheerful. I'm unsure how one manages that state of being when only a short while ago, her husband tried to not only swindle me but also Isabelle. I'm now seeing where Amelie inherited her resilience from.

Today has not been easy on any of us, less for me, way more so for them. I'm not losing money. My dad may be a dick, but at least he doesn't attempt to hide his personality, unlike Noah Boudreaux.

We walk out of the bathroom. Isa doesn't stop in her steps. The words she wants to say are written all over her face. An awe-like expression, happy that I've helped her girl. Since our sneaking around didn't go unnoticed by Isa, I can only hope the other workers at the Inn didn't see us. The only request Amelie had once we started seeing one another at night was to keep things quiet. It worked well for me. My brothers wouldn't care who I'm seeing as long as I'm happy, but the same can't be said for my father, who went so far as to tell me if I don't move my ass back home to New York, I'll be disowned from the family and my trust fund will be dissolved. The threat was just that—a threat. With his next move heading toward presidency, maybe this time, it will be for good. I'd like to say I'm upset, but he's actually doing me a favor. Amelie has to know how pure and sweet her mother is. My own is absolutely not that way. She's more a sheep, willingly following her husband, in essence having zero relationship with me because of it. Thank Christ our child will be in luck in having a grandmother like Isa.

"Hey, Mom. Thank you. I'm not sure I'll be able to keep the toast down, but I'll try the tea." It's on the tip of my tongue to ask if there's caffeine in it but stop myself at the look Amelie is giving me behind her mother's back.

"That's fine. Maybe you'll feel better after a nap. There's probably some kind of virus running its course, or food poisoning? Wait, when's the last time you ate out? You've been home a lot more recently, and no one else is sick, so it must be a virus." I hold back my laughter, ready to make a remark that the only course running through Amelie's system is my child, and it's going to last for at least the first trimester, which I know thanks to the books Parker leaves lying around at his house, subtle hints he's given Nessa he wants to start trying for a family. Never would I have thought I'd be a father before him. Life works in mysterious ways.

"Nope, I've been eating at home. Well, except for the beignets and café au lait the other day," she replies while walking toward where her mother set the tray on the small table in the corner. Beside the table is a chair. Amelie rarely uses it, or she doesn't when I'm here, preferring to sit outside on the small balcony, not caring if it's one hundred plus degrees. She likes what she likes—sunshine and warmth.

"Hmm, well, I guess it's a wait-and-see game. All the same, stay up here today. No need giving it to others in case it's a virus." Isa places her hand on Amelie's cheek, then her forehead.

"Call me if you need anything, though I'm sure Boston will handle things."

"Alright. And, Mom, I can take care of myself. I've been sick before, you know." I guess Amelie isn't ready to tell her mom the truth yet. She's going to have to soon. My plans include a fuck of a lot more than only being a father to our child.

"I know, but accepting help doesn't hurt every once in a while, either. Boston, take care of our girl for me, please." Isabelle walks toward me to squeeze my hand, then leaves as fast as she came. Neither Amelie or I say a word, waiting until her mother is completely out of earshot. My eyes watch as she takes her first sip of tea while my hand reaches into my pocket, wraps around my phone, and bring it up to place a call.

"Don't you dare. I realize she's family to you, but this concerns the two of us first. I'm not telling my mother until I've had an appointment, and since I already have a gynecologist who is also an obstetrician, I've got it covered."

"Then I suggest you make the call now, get the appointment by today, or I'll be taking over whether you like it or not. As much as my money was an issue for you earlier, set it aside. There's no reason a pregnant woman should be fainting. I'm sure you ate last night. It's only going on ten in the morning, and the weather isn't the issue. New Orleans is cooler than it usually is this time of year." She takes another sip of the tea, narrowing her gaze above the dainty teacup. I'd probably break it by setting it down, and I'm sure it's an heirloom.

"You know, I don't particularly care for you right now." The paleness is gone, she's no longer looking green around the gills, and there's that saucy side of her shining through.

"That's okay. You will later when I'm fucking that attitude out of you." That effectively shuts her up. She takes her cup of tea with her as she spins around and heads for the balcony. One thing is for certain: Amelie can run, but she can't hide.

NINE

Amelie

"WHY DOES HE THINK EVERYTHING CAN BE cured with an orgasm?" I mutter to myself, taking my seat on one of the small bistro chairs I have set up on the balcony. Thankfully, my stomach isn't rolling with the urge to purge the small amount of tea I drank. Now, my emotions, sickness, it all makes sense. Chalk it up to the pregnancy and making me feel things I've never felt before. I close my eyes, inhaling the scents coming from down the streets. The spices in the gumbo, jambalaya, and crawfish are hitting already. It figures this child of mine would hate breakfast foods when I absolutely adore any and every item on any given menu to start the day.

"You're going to need this in order to make an appointment with your doctor." The man of the hour walks out, interrupting my tirade right as I was getting ready to blame him and his super sperm for making me the way I am—annoyed, horny, happy, then confused all in a matter of minutes.

"Thank you, Captain Obvious. I was trying to drink my tea before it got cold, but I'll do it now. Clearly, you've got zero patience." And now I'm going to need to add bratty to the list. It's funny how you can miss a person, then suddenly, they're back in your life. You would think it'd be the happiest day in your life when all you want to do is rewind the clock, get some sleep, and start over.

"Nope, not when it comes to you and our child. Amelie, there are only a handful of people I care about in my life. You're one of them, probably more than my brothers and their significant others. I'm going to worry, more so now. You fainted, beautiful, full-blown body trying to drop down to the ground, then, when you're coherent, you tell me you're pregnant. I'm allowed to be concerned. Please make the call." I take my phone from him and place it on the table. Boston sits down in the chair opposite of me, his big body dwarfing the balcony and the chair.

"I've already made the call. I made an appointment after my test came back positive. It's for later this afternoon. And while I can understand your concern, is it possible to, I don't know, maybe talk instead of order me around in the future?"

"Well, I stand corrected." He crosses his arms over his chest, leaning back in the chair. He still doesn't apologize, which is fine by me because I won't either. Being bitchy is absolutely warranted.

"I'll say." My tea is gone, and the queasiness is finally gone, too. My mom and her intuition. Add a little creole on the side, and Isabelle LeBlanc Boudreaux probably has a sneaking suspicion on my being pregnant.

"Still, Amelie, I'll be there. You get that I'm here to stay. We've got a lot of shit to work through, but we're making this work. Shit, beautiful, if I had it my way, we'd have done things a fuck of a lot faster, including you being tied to me in a permanent way. I don't deserve that, not yet. When the time is right and you're not ready to upchuck the contents of your stomach, we'll talk, hash things out, figure out a solid game plan, one that doesn't have you pissed as hell." Boston drops his forearms to his spread thighs, eyes staying on me the entire time he's talking. This man right here, he's the one I gave more than my body to, even if I shouldn't have. The heart wants what the heart wants, and my heart wants Boston. Any way I can have him.

"Yeah, well, going silent for a month wasn't the right way either, you know." Jesus, I need to insert my foot in my mouth. I close my eyes and take a deep breath. Attempting to keep quiet is easier said than done.

"Amelie." He says my name quietly, garnering my attention yet again. "You get who my father is. There was no way I wanted him to catch wind of the woman I've been spending my time with. Do you know what he would have done to you? Your father looks like a joke next to mine. Christ, I couldn't have that. I needed a plan in place. Ezra needed the heat taken off his woman, and I'd already been down here. Theo is in California, both of us taking Four Brothers in a different direction, a necessity to stay fresh in the technology world. I found you, and keeping you safe, far away from Governor Wescott, was all I could think about. I worked night and day. My phone could have been hacked into if I so much as made the wrong move. It wasn't right, but it wasn't wrong either. Hopefully, one day soon, you'll understand what you mean to me," he drops an atomic bomb in my lap. I'm sitting here stunned into silence. I should get up, go to him, at least hug him. Of course, that's not what I do; the simple thing to do slips away from me. Instead, I watch as he stands up from his seat, phone in hand, and walks toward me. "I'm going to grab your toast, make a few phone calls, then I'll be back." The kiss he drops on my lips when I look up as his presence looms over me, well, yeah, I still haven't found the words necessary to respond.

"Okay." It comes out on a croak.

"Alright, you and me, Amelie. We're going to make this work," are his parting words. My stomach somersaults for another reason. Three times today I've had to calm myself down in one form or the other. Though, this one might be my favorite yet, a close second to the desire Boston illuminates in my body whenever we're pressed against one another. I listen as he opens the door, steps inside, and grabs the plate my mom brought up. I know there's butter and cream cheese, a concoction I've always loved on one of my favorite breakfast foods. He sets down the plate, then closes the door as he goes back inside this time, leaving me to contemplate what to make of this new life of mine. One thing is for sure: I'm calling Eden as soon as I'm done eating.

TEN

Boston

"GROUND RULES. I CAN SEE YOU'RE GOING TO BE the type of man who attempts to bulldoze a path of destruction should you not get your way," Amelie tells me as Scott navigates our way to her doctor's appointment hours later. I made a few calls, one to Parker, asking him to set up a conference call with the rest of our brothers since everyone is going every which way. Tomorrow morning, we'll all hop on the call, and I'll tell them what's going on, figuring more will be ironed out after this appointment. Amelie's nerves as well as mine will be a little more settled.

"Go on." Little does she know rules are meant to be broken, and I'll never be the one to agree to them. Though, there's no harm in her thinking she'll get her way.

"First, I'm going to ask the questions and receive the answers before you attempt to stampede your way in like a herd of elephants. Also, while we're on the topic, no bringing up the fact that I've been sick when smelling certain aromas. It's normal, and so is fainting." Scott coughs attempting to cover his laugh, while I'm seething inside with Amelie thinking it's okay to conk out ice fucking cold.

"Wow, you think highly of me. I'm being compared to a bulldozer and an elephant. It's a good thing I don't have any insecurities. I'll agree to you asking the questions first. Should you not ask the ones I'd like answers to, I'll go from there. As for you passing the hell out, that will absolutely be brought to the doctor's attention." Amelie huffs and turns her head away from me when only moments ago, she had no problem giving me those pretty green orbs. Parker warned me what it would be like when I found the one who'd make me fall. Ezra, too, for that matter. Both of them found their life partner. Nessa and Millie are best friends; they also have an independence streak a mile wide. It seems Amelie is right there with them. She can be pissed all she wants. If the mother of my child can't protect herself, I'll be doing it for her.

"Whatever, Boston." The sad part of this equation is I'm at a disadvantage. What started out as a fling of sorts has vastly changed. Having a child together will do that, though our relation-

ship started changing well before I found out she
was pregnant. The late nights started creeping
earlier into the afternoons, I lingered in the
morning, and we exchanged texts during the
time I was in New Orleans. It was only when I
went back to New York that things got dicey.
Unfortunately, Amelie doesn't know just how
cruel Governor Wescott can and will be, no
matter the fact he disowned me a few days ago.

"Amelie." Her name comes out as a grumble.
My hand moves to where hers lies between us.
The good news is, when I lock our fingers
together, she doesn't pull away. "I'm not some
overbearing dick. Can we at least agree that
when it comes to your health, questions need to
be asked? What if it happened while you were
working?" Amelie and Isa pull their weight at
the Inn. No task is too menial—cleaning
windows, scrubbing toilets, washing laundry.
The two of them work alongside the employees
to take care of the daily tasks. They don't act
like pompous assholes while watching the people
they hired work harder than they do.

"Fine. Don't get used to me saying this, but
you're right in that regard," she admits, unwill-
ingly. We're saved from further conversation
when Scott pulls up to the hospital where her
doctor's office is located, a two-for-one deal. I'm
happier about it, too. If there's a problem, well,
she can be escorted safely in a wheelchair or
hospital bed to the next floor.

"Thank you. I didn't get to ask with all the phone calls I had to field. Is your doctor a male or female?" I question. My calls didn't take too long. Parker was the fastest. I laid it out about the building and then asked for him to set up a good time for the guys to receive a call all at once. I made another call to my realtor, where I relayed the information about the building. How I managed to remain calm is anyone's guess, when all I wanted to do was fire her on the spot. The mistake may have been an honest one; it still didn't sit well with me. Adding that Amelie and her mother could have been hurt in the process only makes it that much worse. Needless to say, the company now knows what will and won't be tolerated. Margaret Smith is currently working on finding another building, this one not being sold out from beneath an unsuspecting family. And if I have my way, it'll happen immediately. Time is of the essence in my line of work.

"Oh, dear God, you did not ask that question. Is your job to piss me off today?" She tries to snatch her hand away. I don't allow that to happen, keeping it firmly in place with mine.

With her hand still in mine, I pull her closer, "Not particularly. I do enjoy when you bring all that feistiness to the bedroom, though."

"Shut up, Boston." There's no anger or annoyance in her tone. Pregnancy hormones are working in my favor.

"Answer the question, beautiful."

"My doctor is a female, but I wouldn't switch if she were a male. You would have to get used to the fact that another man is looking at something you've already had." The lust between us passes as we make our way to the hospital entrance, and the sliding doors open automatically.

"Don't test me, Amelie. There's only so much a man can take, and I'm so damn close to taking you to the bathroom, bending you over, and fucking that sauciness out of you, in turn making us late to your first obstetrician appointment, would be frowned upon." She's saved from responding when we have to go through the metal detectors. Her "Whatever" under her breath is the only response I receive. Now I'm the one left with the issue of my cock hardening with the visual I've described. Of course, it doesn't stop there. It's been too fucking long since we've had one another, and that's going to change. Today.

ELEVEN

Amelie

"I THINK GIVING THEM A KIDNEY WOULD BE easier than all the paperwork I had to fill out." The elevator ride up to the fifth floor was done in silence with more people in the small space than I'd like. Boston had me pressed to his front, filling my senses with his scent and presence, especially the one poking me in my backside. It was nice to know I wasn't the only one who is affected when he's nearby. I finish the last piece of paper of what seemed like an inch thick of paperwork. My family history was a breeze to get through. I wasn't expecting Boston to answer it with ease. I should never assume anything when it comes to the man sitting beside me. He's quite literally thrown me for a loop each and every time.

"No kidding. You'd think with all the papers they take in, the hospital would switch to an electronic questionnaire of sorts or ask you to do it online before you come." He takes the clipboard from my hands, his lips grazing my forehead as he stands. I could cry with the way he handles me and this current situation. One minute I'm pissed off, at what? Nothing, literally nothing. Sure, the man went silent. I get it; he was protecting me. It still hurt, and there's so much left unsaid. Me falling pregnant isn't really helping matters. The other minute, I'm riddled with desire, ready to tear our clothes off and ride his face, fingers, or cock, or all three, preferably the first two at the same time, the remaining orgasm being left for Boston's thickness. Then there's another part of me which is ready to break down and cry buckets of tears. Mental headcase is what I'm going with. It's not a diagnosis, but it should be, for me at least. I'm sure other pregnant women don't go through this, right? I watch as Boston walks to the reception desk. Gone is his jacket. He still remains in the suit, black long-sleeve shirt tucked in, black pants that showcase his firm ass and thick thighs, and once again, he's setting off a desire inside me that needs to stay locked up until after this appointment.

"Amelie Boudreaux," my name is called out. Boston turns around, and I watch the entire process as fierce protectiveness is written all over him. I nod, mouthing, *I'm okay. This is normal.* Either he really is right about his father, or the man has another worry, one he hasn't spoken about.

"Hi," I tell the nurse, stepping toward her.

"Hi, this will only take a minute. We're going to do a urinalysis, then we'll call you back to a room once it's run and a room is available," she explains. I feel Boston's arm slide around my lower back.

"Thank you." I take a step to follow her, feeling Boston take a step with me. "Boston, I'll be right back."

"Where are you going?" he responds,

"To pee in a cup. You can't come with me." I'm sure my cheeks are flush with color. The look he gives me, the cocking of an eyebrow, the uplift of his lip are all too telling. The man absolutely would follow me to the restroom and watch me pee in the most un-lady like manner if I'd let him.

"I can, Amelie, don't test me on that. Go take care of your business. I'll stand here and wait for you." So much for stopping him from walking to the back of the office. The man is really going to stand outside the bathroom door, hearing me pee, fiddle with a specimen cup, and give me zero space. Jesus, what did I sign myself up for?

"Don't worry, honey, he's not the first one to do this. He won't be the last." The nurse hands me what I need. I huff out another breath of air, feeling like I'm a teenager in a snit about my curfew. Boston chuckles and mans his post. I ignore him. Damn alpha male pride; he's really testing my will to live today. Of course, in my tirade, I try to open the restroom door with attitude. It doesn't work out well for me with it being on a hinge and all; my dramatic ass is shown up by none other than wood. The automatic lights flicker on, and the door closes softly behind me. I roll my eyes. I'm well aware of the breath I'm holding, mainly because I'm trying to relax. Who knew going pee with the father of your child standing so close to door would give you stage freight? Me, that's who. I release my breath. There's no time like the present. I ignore the mirror. There's no way I'm going to look at myself. Today has been a day, almost like a Monday, except it's not. It's just a normal day. I should be doing normal things. Morning sickness, fainting, telling Boston he's going to be a father, dealing with my own father, yeah, it's been one of those days.

I do what needs to be done as I follow the instructions that are printed in bold print right in front of the toilet, trying to block out the outside noise that comes through, going so far as to hum to hurry this along. A few moments later, the specimen cup is in the metal container that has a door on each side wedged between the walls, I'm washing my hands, and then I'm out the door.

"Everything okay?" Boston asks the loaded question.

"Your room is already available. I'm going to take your vitals, then the doctor will be in with you shortly." The nurse saves the day from me word-vomiting all over Boston and how annoyed I am at the slightest provocation. We follow her into the next alcove. "First, we'll take your weight, blood pressure, and temperature." Without being told, Boston turns around, hands in his pockets. I'm thankful for one thing going my way. I was really worried my mouth was going to run away with me should he exert his dominance in watching how this whole thing goes down. I kick off my shoes. They probably don't weigh a lot as it is, but every little bit helps. The nurse types it on her laptop, then I step off.

"You can turn around now," I tell Boston, then sit down while she pulls the small cart from the corner, takes out the thermometer, places the probe beneath my tongue, and then takes my blood pressure. The cuff really does hurt as she pumps it full of air. My eyes are seeing stars. Boston must realize something is going to happen because the last thing I notice is him rushing toward me, hands cradling my head, before darkness consumes me.

TWELVE

Boston

"THIS BETTER BE A NORMAL SIDE EFFECT OF pregnancy," I state to the doctor, unable to keep the worry from my tone. If this happens naturally, well, this will be the last child Amelie has. I'll get a fucking vasectomy the second our child is born. My heart still hasn't recovered as she returns to consciousness on the bed in the room her nurse pointed me toward. Carrying her wasn't a hardship, and it was faster than the nurse, now known as Stacy, to get a wheelchair.

"Boston, stop being so grouchy and let Dr. Dana talk for a minute," Amelie says as if she wasn't conked out only moments ago.

"This can be very normal during your first trimester of pregnancy. A drop in blood pressure, low sugar levels, it can be a domino effect in her fainting spells. What's the last thing you had to eat?"

"Tea and toast earlier this morning." Dr. Dana hums in response, looking over her chart on the laptop. I'm tempted to call Ezra and ask him to hack into the hospital and give me all of Amelie's reports, find a doctor of my choice, preferably one I can fly in from New York to get the real answers.

"That could have a lot to do with it. Are you feeling any dizziness, nausea, vomiting?" I snort, trying to keep my mouth shut while the two of them talk, but knowing Amelie, she'll try and shrug it off.

"Nausea, definitely. The smell of eggs has me rolling." She leaves off the other important parts.

"She fainted earlier today, and not so much vomiting. Dry heaving, yes, but she had nothing to get up." Amelie's gaze shifts to me.

"There is that, too," she finally admits to the doctor exactly what happened.

"Ah, okay. Well, morning sickness, unable to keep food or liquids down, can result in your sugar and blood pressure dropping. I'm going to prescribe you an anti-nausea medicine to take as needed. A lot of expectant mothers keep crackers and a lemon-lime soda of sorts on their nightstand, swearing they eat it before their feet touch the ground helps a lot. Now, judging by your last menstrual cycle, you're about seven weeks along. Would you like to hear your child's heartbeat?" Amelie's face gets soft. Part of the questionnaire she had to answer was about her options and what she'd like to choose. I watched out of the corner of my eye, a churning in my gut at the potential of her changing her mind. It eased when she put a check mark by *childbirth*.

"Yes, and yes to the medicine, but I'm also going to try the cracker and soda route first. This guy will no doubt hover over me for the next however many months."

"Wrong. Try years, Amelie. I'm not going anywhere, not today, not tomorrow, not ever, and not because you're the mother of our child either." Amelie's eyes fill with tears. It doesn't matter that we're in a room with her doctor; she needed to hear with her own ears that I'm not leaving her. She's it for me, and once a few things are cleared between us, she'll hear the words I once told her while she was sleeping.

"Alright, well, let's get to it, then. I'm going to step out for a few moments. We still need to do a pelvic exam, as well as the doppler to hear the baby's heartbeat. Your next appoint, we'll do a transvaginal ultrasound, measure a few things. I'll be seeing you once a month as long as your morning sickness and fainting don't get worse. Also, I'd like you to monitor your blood pressure twice a day, to err on the side of safety." Dr. Dana stands up from her stool, pulls out a cotton gown and a sheet for Amelie before leaving so she can get changed. This time, I won't be leaving the room. Seeing her naked is a sight I'm going to enjoy even if it is in an office building where we can't take things any further.

"Thank you," I tell her.

"I won't take long. Thank you for explaining everything." I make a mental note to ask Parker to send me the title and author of the pregnancy book he keeps in the living room, hopeful Vanessa will catch on to his tactics. I've yet to hit the halfway point in the book. If only I had finished it, I probably would have seen the writing on the wall and known what to look for all along.

"That's what I'm here for. I'll be back in a few minutes." Dr. Dana leaves the room. I sit back in my chair, knowing if I offer to help Amelie off the table, she'll give me a scornful look, and I'd rather she uses what energy she does have left on other things, like when we're in bed tonight.

"You're enjoying this, aren't you?" I lick my lips, choosing not to respond, keeping a watchful eye on her as she kicks off her shoes. Her hands go to the bottom of her shirt, and one inch at a time, bare smooth skin is shown, until she pulls it over her head, leaving her in a deep purple lace bra and shorts.

"I am, though it sucks I can't take advantage of the situation. I will once we're back at the Inn." I recline in my seat and spread my legs further, giving myself room as the blood rushes to my cock. She shimmies out of her shorts, taking what I'm sure is a matching lace thong off along the way. Christ, she's beautiful. Amelie watches as my hand goes to my lap, situating myself in a way she can see exactly what she does to me. It doesn't matter if she's clothed or naked like she is now, though I wouldn't mind if she flicked the clasp on her bra.

"Oh, is that so? And am I asked or being told?" She does what I want without being told, arm moving behind her back. I lick my lips. Her tits are the perfect handful. Now that she's completely bare, I can see the first sign of a subtle change. Her breasts are fuller, nipples a deeper color, and damn do want them in my hands. My mouth waters at the thought of wrapping my lips around the pebbled tips. "Boston." My hand grazes her lower abdomen, moving until my thumb is pressed against her clit, hating that I can't take this further. It wouldn't take long at all to get her off. Feeling her tremble beneath me is a vision that stayed stored with me. Anytime I'd jack off, it was to Amelie, whether it was to a fantasy I want to play out with her or one of the multiple times we were together. Whichever it was, it guaranteed to have me coming in no time, in the shower, in bed. Fuck, as long as it's Amelie, that's all that matters.

I pull my hand away reluctantly. "Christ, Amelie, I didn't think you could taste any sweeter," I tell her after bringing my thumb to my mouth, licking off her essence. Her thighs clench. "Beautiful, that's a promise, and you can guarantee I'll be at each of these appointments, especially after today's striptease. Get your gown on, Amelie. We probably only have a minute left until the doctor's knocking on the door." I grimace at losing the sight as well as the feel of her body.

"I hope you make good on your promise, Boston." She turns around. I hiss when her peach-shaped ass is on full display. The palm of my hand is itching to smack her ass the way she likes when I have her bent over any piece of furniture we make it to, and when she bends down to pick up the clothes she dropped, the view is incredible. Sadly, it's gone way too fast. She folds them quickly and puts them on the counter next to the table, then comes the gown, taking away the sight of her naked body. It might be a good thing, too, because without my suit jacket, hiding my hard cock isn't going to be easy.

"I always deliver, Amelie." The knock and then the door opening closes our conversation down. It's time to hear our child's heartbeat.

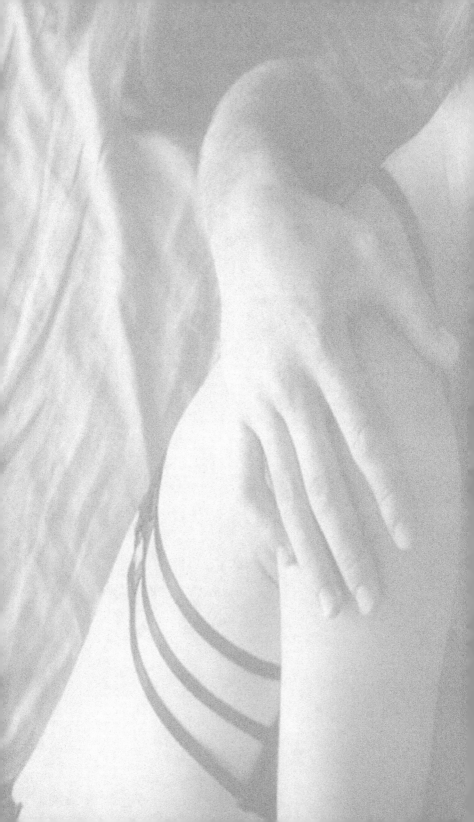

THIRTEEN

Amelie

I WAKE UP IN MY BED, EYES GOING STRAIGHT TO where I last saw Boston. His laptop was out, iPad on his lap, and phone to his ear as he talked in hushed tones to whom I have no idea. All I know is, after hearing our baby's heartbeat, I was crying happy tears, so lost in my emotions that my arm went over my eyes, shielding Boston and the doctor while also using it to soak up all the freaking wetness coating my cheeks. It didn't work. Boston was right there beside me, pulling my arm away from my face while the rapid beating of our child's heart is echoing through the room. Well, I'd put it up there with the top three noises that stick with you forever. Once his eyes locked on mine, a soft smile coming out to play, my own heart sputtered for a whole different reason. I was so close to blurting out a sentence, one with three words, starts with an *I* and ends with a *u*. Boston wiped the tears from my face, cupping my cheeks and using his thumbs in a different way than he had earlier. I can't even imagine the next time my appointment rolls around, to see our baby flutter around, hear his or her heartbeat once again. I'm going to be a bundle of emotions. There are no two ways about it, and with Boston stating he'd be at every appointment, he will be subjected to my emotional upheavals.

After the appointment, where he refused to let me pay my own co-pay, we scheduled my next checkup around lunch time, Boston so in tune with my work, staying busy in the morning and afternoons. Cleaning rooms, making sure food and drinks are out in the lobby, then checking in new guests. It makes for a weird system to regulate your life around. How my mother has managed to do it all her life, I have no idea. All I know is that if she can do it, so can I, even if a baby is strapped to my chest. A loud grumble came from my stomach. Clearly, the nausea had settled down, and a hunger like no other took its place. Scott was idling at the entrance to the hospital. Boston told him to head back to the area of the Inn; we'd walk to lunch. There wasn't a whole lot of persuading me with that idea. The only thing I asked for was jambalaya; the spicy rice, sausage, and shrimp meal was calling my name. The buttery bread the restaurant paired with it was exactly what I needed, until I saw what Boston ordered. His shrimp 'po boy' had me looking longingly at his meal. Being the gentlemen he is, we shared our meals. The best of both worlds in my eyes, during the perfect time of day, where you can sit outside, watch the people come and go. The wait for our food wasn't long, and the slight breeze helped keep us cool. A few yawns later, Boston asked for the check. I tried to slide cash for my food across the table, but one look at his jawline told me he wasn't having it, so I reluctantly tucked my money away in my wallet. Next time we go somewhere, I'll have to figure out a way to pay him back. I finished my orange juice, well aware of the fact that spicy food mixed with an acidic drink was asking for a heartburn later. Totally worth it at the time.

Since Scott dropped us off, Boston relieved him for the day, and we walked hand in hand back to the Inn. Mom was busy in another part of the hotel. We used the back stairs to head up to my room. I assumed we would go our separate ways then, but Boston, like usual, did what I least expected. He told me to slip into something more comfortable while he was going to grab his laptop bag and work while I rested. Which is where we are now. True to his word, Boston is sitting in the chair in the corner, the side table pulled in front of him, crouched over his laptop, iPad set up off to the side, phone held up to his ear with one hand while he scratches at a notepad beneath the palm of his hand. What

I'm not expecting are the black-rimmed glasses he has propped on the bridge of his nose. Just when I thought he couldn't get any hotter, there he goes, adding another layer. My thighs clench, and a low moan leaves my lips. I watch as his eyes snap to mine. When I changed out of my clothes, it was into my pajamas from last night, a satin emerald-green spaghetti strap with lace on each side and a deep V in the front; the same pattern is carried through to the shorts.

"I'll call you back, Theo. Something's come up." My body lights up. His eyes stay on mine when he tosses the phone on top of his work, hand coming up to do the same to his glasses, and a look of pure unadulterated lust is written all over his face. I watch as he stands. His shirt sleeves are rolled up, showing off his muscular forearms, and a few buttons are undone at his throat, giving me a view of his upper chest. He's giving me my own personal porn show. "Sleep well, beautiful?" he asks as he makes his way toward me. My mouth waters, nipples pebbling further, and it's not from the air conditioning he currently has blasting through my room. I'm sure part of the reason I slept so well was due to how cold it currently is. With it only being me in here most of the time, I keep it kicked up a few more degrees than most. Add in that little sleep happened last night, plus a play on more emotions in twenty-four hours than I've experienced in my whole life all at once. And then there's Boston. To say I'm addicted to his presence would be putting it mildly. When he's around, my guard drops. I don't think about my father and his shenanigans, worrying about what he's up to next. It all fades away. Boston is the only one who can keep the wolves at bay, so to speak.

"Really well. Work hard while I was being a lady of leisure?" I was half expecting to wake up nauseous. Eggs, eggs are the freaking culprit. How am I going to wake up each morning, work, and deal with getting sick from the smell of Mom cooking breakfast? Or God forbid I'm relegated to the kitchen to take on the task. The thought alone makes me want to cry.

"As much as I could since you were in this big bed alone." His deft fingers start working the buttons of his shirt, flicking one open with every step he takes.

"You could have joined me." Screw communicating. I'd rather do a different kind of talking, one with our bodies.

"I'm going to now, starting with an afternoon snack." I flip back the covers. My back is to the headboard, legs spread open, giving Boston all the invitation he needs. And lucky me, this time, *I'm* getting a striptease.

FOURTEEN

Boston

I watch as Amelie gives me the view of a motherfucking lifetime. The only problem is, she's wearing entirely too many clothes even if her satin pajamas still show of a good amount of skin. I want her bare, legs spread, pussy on full display for me before I taste her sweetness. I strip off my shirt and pants while making my way toward her. Might have been the smartest thing I've done besides knocking Amelie up.

"Look at you, wet and ready for me. I know exactly how I'm going to make up for being gone, starting with tasting your cunt, then working my way up to your nipples. I know how much you like me sucking on them until your pussy pulses with need, on the brink of coming. Then I'm going to give you my cock, feeling your cunt ripple around my length. Fuck yeah, Amelie. I'm going to do everything to you." I

95

prowl. Let's be realistic, I'm crawling up the bed, on my hands and knees for Amelie and only Amelie. She spreads her thighs further apart. My eyes rove her entire body, unable to land on one solid place—the pursing of her lips as she tries to hold her composure, her eyes that are full of want and desire, chest heaving, nipples pebbled beneath her top. I remember how she whimpers when my teeth bite down on the tips.

"Oh God." Her voice is throaty, desperation laced through each syllable. The front of my legs meet the back of her thighs. I'm sitting on my haunches, hands sliding up her smooth legs, watching as a shiver races up her body. I'm usually one to take my time, but that's a luxury that isn't happening this first round. I hook my thumbs at her waist and tear down her bottoms. Fuck the top. Next round, I'll tear it off her, or I'll have her lift the scant piece of fabric while I play with her tits.

"One taste, then I'll give you what you want." I wrap my hands around the outside of her thighs, move backwards, and dip my head. Amelie's scent goes straight to my head, intoxicating me in so many ways, it's mouthwatering. It's been too damn long. A long languid lick along her slit, dipping my tongue inside the place my cock is dying to be. Who am I kidding? I want more. One taste will never be enough when it comes to Amelie. The tip of my tongue plays with her clit, tracing where she's currently got the back of my head secured, so I can't move, or so she thinks.

"Boston, don't you dare tease me, not today." My shoulders hold her thighs open. Wetness is dripping from her bare pussy. A moan rumbles from my chest. It's been too damn long since I've had her like this. My thumb slides inside her heat. Her begging me not to tease was easy in my book. I'm too far gone, already knowing once her first orgasm is over, I'll be fucking my cock inside, and this time without a condom. My cock drips with precum, a multitude of factors coming in to play—the clamping of her thighs around my head, holding me hostage, the way her greedy pussy clamps around my digit, how she's rocking her body back and forth.

"Fuck yes," I breathe into her center when she let's go. It's a beautiful sight. Her eyes are closed, body arched up in a way that you know she's offering herself to me while holding me hostage at the same time, right where she wants me. I slowly bring her down, my fingers leaving her entrance, tongue slowly laving at her clit. My cock is pissed as hell at me for not taking what he wants, instead allowing her to have an orgasm. Clearly, Amelie isn't the only insatiable one. I lift up, moving until I'm back where this all started, cock hard, precum leaking from the tip.

"Guide me in, beautiful." Her eyes flash open, soft and dreamy, as I tell her what to do. A hiss leaves me when I feel her soft hand envelope my length. "Christ, can't take much more. I need to be inside you." She places me right where I need to be. The head of my cock is happy to be inside her. My eyes close. The temptation to ram right in is there. The only thing holding me back is myself. If I were to do that, I'd more than likely come before I'm ready, and my woman deserves more than a one-minute man.

"Boston." My name is a soft mewl. I drop to my hands, her own on my arms, muscles bulging, and I slide in further.

"Eyes, Amelie, I want them on me while my cock fucks you." She spasms around me, and I'm not even all the way inside. What the hell is she going to do once the entirety of her heat is clutching me is anybody's guess.

"Then quit messing around." Her feet that are planted on the mattress help propel her hips up. One orgasm clearly wasn't enough. I don't deny her the satisfaction of holding her off. I'm too far gone, needing to rut inside her like a fucking dog in heat. "Yes, God, yes, right there." I bottom out. She takes my entire length. My body locks up, trying to hold back the sensation of taking her without a condom. Nobody, not one single person, could have prepared me for all the feelings that are rolling through my body.

"Amelie." Holding back is no longer an option. I thrust my hips backward and forward. She meets me with each movement. My perfect fucking match, Amelie is mine, and the baby she's growing inside of her is mine, too.

"Boston." Her voice mirrors the need in my own. This time when we come, it's together, with no barrier between us, and fuck does she make me want to be a better version of myself.

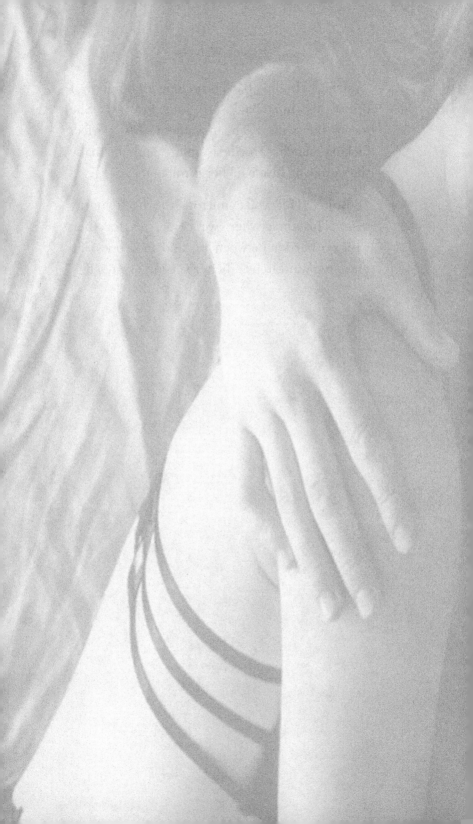

FIFTEEN

Amelie

———

BOSTON AND I DIDN'T COME UP FOR AIR AFTER he joined me in bed late yesterday afternoon, wearing me out in a way that the two-hour nap didn't stop me from sleeping through the night. How did he manage that? Well, three orgasms, first trimester pregnancy sleepiness, and him curling his body around mine was all it took, causing me to pass out. Of course, when we woke up, it was to the smell of my mother's cooking. My stomach rolled, but Boston saved the day yet again. There, on the nightstand, were the soda, saltine crackers, and the prescription he somehow had filled without my knowledge. Another point in my book because I absolutely needed it. After I got to a point where the contents of my stomach were settled down, Boston kissed me goodbye and left to meet with his realtor.

"Okay, never again are you allowed to give me shit. Who is the one who went two days without FaceTiming whom now?" my best friend Eden says on the other end of the line. She called me earlier today, but I couldn't answer. It killed me not to. I needed to talk to her, cleanse my soul and get things off my chest. But since I didn't pull my weight yesterday at the Inn, it was time to get my ass in gear as soon as the queasiness subsided. I've yet to still tell my mother what's going on. Eden is first, then my mom. We just won't tell her that's how it went. Now there's a lull in work, everyone is settled for the time being, and Mom is out running an errand, giving me the time I need to talk to my bestie.

"I suck, or rather, I should have, and I wouldn't be pregnant," I drop a bombshell of an answer on her. It wasn't long ago that we were talking about how I'd never find a man like she has. My, my, how the tides have turned.

"Um, excuse me? You want to rewind what you said to me?" The shock on her face, tipped with a smile, she's not playing anyone in this friend-ship. College roomies turned long distance besties, we've been through a lot together.

"I'm pregnant?" I play dumb, smiling proudly into the screen. I'm sitting outside. The street below is bustling with people. The only worry I had was if Eden would scream through the phone. Thankfully, she didn't, so no one is going to call the cops with how loud Eden can be in a state of excitement.

"Wow, okay. Well, Boston sure knows how to make his sperm count. You're going to have to tell me every single thing because he's been gone for a month. Is he back now? Are you excited? Does he know? Does your mom know? Do you need me and Samuel to come down there?" Leave it to Eden to slam me with questions. Here goes nothing. She'll know every single thing after I catch her up on the life that is Amelie.

"Yeah, he left me with a parting gift. He's back in New Orleans. For good. I'm so freaking excited. We got to hear the baby's heartbeat yesterday. Neither of us had dry eyes, me less than Boston, but you get it. I blurted out that I was pregnant after I fainted. I'm good now, though. Eggs make me hug certain apparatuses, like we did after day drinking, which sucks. Still worth it, though. I'm telling you, then Mom next, and you two are always welcome down here, but not to kick anyone's ass. Unless you count my dad's. In that case, I kind of wish Kavanaugh were still a lawyer and he could fuck with him, wear Dad down enough that he'd go away forever." I go into the fiasco of yesterday morning, telling her about how I found Boston there on the street, feeling like my world exploded when in all reality, it was dumb luck and a case of Noah Boudreaux being scum of the earth. I know you're supposed to love your family unconditionally; nope, that is no longer an option. Eden takes a sip of her coffee. How she can drink as much caffeine as she does and not have a heart attack, I'll never understand. Ugh, speaking of which. Boston chastised me about the intake of that, too. I promptly ignored him, too busy worrying about my stomach than the coffee I usually gravitate toward.

"Wow, and you thought my relationship was a whirlwind. I'm pretty sure you skipped past what people would call the norm and are going to have an instant family." Kavanaugh sneaks into the screen, pressing a kiss to the side of her head.

"Hey, Amelie," he says.

"Hiya, Kavanaugh," I respond. It's an unspoken rule he's Samuel only to Eden and a handful of others.

"I'm going to grab lunch. Be back soon," he tells Eden.

"Alright, thank you." She watches him head out the door, waiting until the door is shut before saying, "Okay, where were we? I swear that man will one day impregnate me by a look alone." We both giggle. I'm honestly surprised that she isn't pregnant right along with me.

"Well, if that were the case, I'd have been pregnant by Boston the day we met. My goodness, is that man fine." We continue our back-and-forth banter. When she asks if she'll be Aunty Eden as well as the godmother, I roll my eyes at the dumb question. Of course, she will. I have a feeling our child is going to be spoiled with a lot of love, even if my father isn't around. There's plenty of others in our corner, between Eden, Kavanaugh, Boston's brothers, and my mom. I may not know Boston as well as I'd have liked before becoming pregnant, but one thing is for sure: he'd never be the man his father or my father turned out to be.

"Alright, chickee, I've got to grab a quick bite to eat and get back to work. I promise I'll Face-Time you tomorrow." My turkey sandwich, chips, and fruit sit in front of me. Instead of orange juice, today it's water.

"Okay, Samuel will be back soon. Love you, Amelie."

"Love you, too." We hang up, and my hand already reaches for my sandwich. I'm starving for my first meal of the day.

SIXTEEN

Boston

"AND THIS BUILDING IS ACTUALLY BEING SOLD BY the owner?" I ask my realtor. Unlike Amelie and Isabelle, Margaret Smith isn't a native. Like me, she's a transplant from another area. A few hours into our appointment and four buildings later, this one finally has potential. The first one was more rubble and less concrete, and we didn't even take a step into the last one before I told her it wasn't happening. No way am I going to sink my money into something with potentially little to no profit when other variables are in the mix, outgrowing one site and needing a bigger business front, or should the reverse happen, the business sink like a ship out at sea with two hurricanes hovering around them. I'm not expecting that to happen. Four Brothers has yet to fail at any of our endeavors. I'll be damned if we do now.

"It is. And by the way, Noah Boudreaux was reported to the police." I'm not holding my breath. It's a known fact in any area of the world, it's not what you know, it's who you know. A slap on the wrist is more than likely the size of it, which sucks for Amelie and her mother. Four Brothers' attorney and friend, Sylvester Sterling, will be making an appearance once there's finally a damn lock on the right place.

"That's good." I shrug my shoulders. The only person that shit hurt is the one who has my gut tied in knots, a domino effect because what hurts her mother, hurts Amelie. "This place isn't bad," I murmur, taking a look at the shell of four concrete walls. The floor is much the same. The metal rafters are in good shape. The size will work, too, with plenty of room to set up multiple office spaces. And at least down in this area, the parking garage is only across the street.

"It's been on the market for nine months. The sellers are ready to off-load it." I look down at the pamphlet and note the price. Even with the renovations and setbacks, it could work out.

"Offer them twenty percent below asking price. We'll see if they're up to negotiate, put the ball in their court." I've already spent way too much time on finding a building. The last time I was down here, a contract fell through, and, well, that was a shit show of epic proportions. At least now that I'm here permanently, I'll be overseeing it in the entirety. No fucking around will be happening, even if I have to bring employees from out of state to get this show on the road.

"I'm willing to try. That's nearly a million below asking price, Mr. Wescott. Are you sure this is the approach you want to take?" Margaret asks. I'm about to fire her, take the middleman out, have Sylvester handle the paperwork and call it a fucking day. This is what I get for being nice, questioned to death, being shown bullshit that she knows won't work but is wanting a quick commission. The phone ringing interrupts the way I feel about my realtor questioning me, and it's not my phone either. I should have stayed with Amelie. Leaving wasn't easy, but she assured me she'd call at the first sign of not feeling okay. I was reluctant, especially when she woke up with a repeat of yesterday's performance, minus passing out. Jesus, Amelie would be in the hospital this time around if that happened.

"If you'll excuse me," Margaret says, taking the phone call.

"Sure." I pull my own phone out of my pocket and walk further into the building as I scroll through the alerts, making sure Amelie hasn't texted. In all honesty, I doubt the mother of my unborn child would ever admit defeat by making a call for help. I go to my phone app, scroll until I find Sylvester' phone number. He's

an extension of our friend group at Four Brothers. Ezra needed him recently; now it's my turn
to call in a few favors. The thing about having a
friend who owns his own law firm is that you're
able to bypass the red tape of a secretary who
will undoubtedly force you to make an appointment. Sly answering on the second ring is
another perk. "Tell me I don't need to bail you
out of jail," he answers the phone.

"Fuck no. I need you to do more of a menial
task than hopping on your company jet, flying
down here, signing a few documents, and
charging me out the ass for a few hours of your
time," I reply, pacing the floors in what will
more than likely become the back office on the
first floor until the others are worked on.

"Jesus, the reason my firm is raking in the
money is from you, Parker, Ezra, and Theo.
What's going on now?" Sly lies like the devil,
charming his opponents in whatever match he
meets, working in a way you'll never see him
coming.

"I'm going to fire this real estate agent. I gave
her a second chance after yesterday's fiasco. I'm
not feeling it today. Four hours, more places
than I'd care to look at when she knew my
guidelines before finally finding one, and she's
questioning what I want to offer. I'll pay her a
fee for her time, but I want you to make the
magic happen. I don't care if it's one of your

other lawyers since I've got you working on other shit. I only need this to happen to-fucking-day." I stuff my hand not holding my phone in the pocket of my pants.

"That won't take but a few minutes. Hold on a minute. I'll get it sorted now, then you can get back to working on what you need to. While we're on the phone, I know you don't want to hear this, but your father is on a fucking tear, so watch your back. I'm handling the front lines, and believe it or not, so is your mother. She came in earlier today, refusing to leave until she got my attention, making a scene and leaving my secretary shocked." Sly shouldn't be surprised on both accounts. My mother can put up a fuss behind closed doors, the soft docile lady leaves and a flaming inferno comes out. An hour long tirade turns into days on end when she's good and pissed. I'd bet she caught my father fucking another election volunteer. Young, blonde, and someone who willingly puts out is his preference. As for Sylvester's secretary, well, all I can say is I'm not sure how she's lasted as long as she has. She's young, naïve, and it's her first job, so I'm at a loss for words why Sly hired her in the first place.

"I take it he didn't like me pulling my money out of the trust fund my grandfather set up for me and putting it into a different bank?" I'm forty-two years old. It's money my mom's father set up for me before he passed away. Leaving it for as long as I did where he could monitor the interest it was earning was dumb on my part.

"Not at all. Your mother came in and asked if I could take a look at her accounts. I told her I'd talk to you before I'd proceed; otherwise, this would be cut and dry. Sterling & Associates has a department that would investigate everything, find whatever it is she is looking for, and go from there. It's up to you, Boston," Sly lays out. Jesus, what is this week coming to? I got the fuck out of New York, trying to take the heat off of Ezra and Millie, and now look what's happening. I'm getting the heat, and my friend has to help more than expected.

"It's up to you. Mr. Governor has the potential to make your life a living hell. I know how you feel about publicity, good or bad. Taking the brunt of Mom's issues only for her to get right back in her old ways. Man, I'm not sure it's smart." The realtor starts to head my way. Son of a bitch. I should have left while on the phone with Sly. It'd be better for him to pay the woman off to keep her off my back. So far, the only good thing that has come from leaving New York is taking the heat off Four Brothers and Amelie. Christ, the scent, the feel, the taste of her body, it's a damn aphrodisiac, shooting straight to your head.

"This is true. I'll take the night to mull it over. In the meantime, shake the realtor loose, send me over the listing, and we'll have the deal closed by tomorrow morning."

"Will do. Thanks, brother," I reply.

"You won't be thanking me when the bill arrives. Talk later." He hangs up the phone. I take another moment to myself, kicking my own ass. I've made a mess of this whole situation. I should have had Sylvester negotiate the entire time. Fuck, I've been down here studying the atmosphere, the culture, wanting to broaden where Four Brothers is going, making rookie mistake after rookie mistake. The only thing I didn't screw up is Amelie. I take that back because I did the entire time I was in New York, leaving her down here without so much as a damn text. Yeah, I've got a lot of stuff to fix, starting with the realtor and trickling down from there.

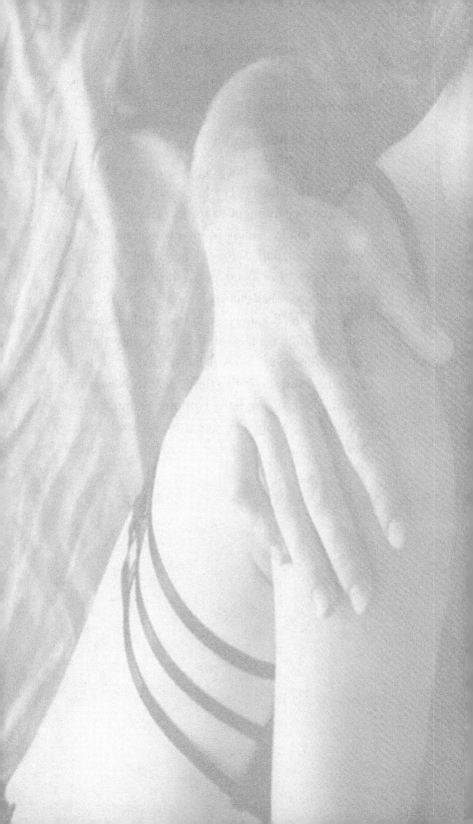

SEVENTEEN

Amelie

"HEY, MOM, DO YOU HAVE A SECOND?" I ASK once the guests checking-in for the evening die down. The niggle in the back of my mind doesn't leave, I should have hunted her down after lunch to tell mom about the impending grandchild she's have this year. Except she was nowhere to be seen. Now, the nausea I'm feeling is not from her cooking breakfast; it's a direct correlation with me spilling my guts in a different way.

"Sure, honey, let's go to the kitchen. I can prep a few things while we talk." Her sleek bob hair-style has a clip at the back of her head, keeping her hair out of her face, and she's wearing light makeup. When you're moving from room to room, hustling like you never have before, you tend to keep things simple. Nobody wants their mascara or lipstick sliding off their face when you're dripping with sweat.

"Alright." I follow her. The polished wood floor is gleaming, the white beige-colored walls reflecting off them. Every piece of furniture is shining, there are fresh flowers from the market in vases, gold accents here and there, and plush leather furniture that's comfortable but also made to last. Mom pushes through the swinging doors. This is where the bulk of the renovations took place. We both wanted to make our guests stay luxurious, and what better way to do that than with breakfast served each morning, buffet style, with drinks and snacks readily available at any time of day, especially fresh chocolate chip cookies? I snag one from the island before taking my seat.

"How are you and Boston doing?" She has her back to me. Both fridge doors are open, the commercial-grade style where you can fit at least four bodies inside. She's probably trying to figure out what to put on the menu tomorrow besides fresh fruit.

"We're good." She turns around at the right time, three cartons of eggs stacked high in her arms. Oh God, the sight alone has me ready to hop off the barstool and run away. "Really good, in fact, but, um, there's something you should know. And can you put the eggs away, please?" I swear if she so much as cracks one egg by accident, I'm going to hurl, and knowing my luck, making it to the nearest bathroom or trashcan won't come close to happening.

"That's great. He came by this morning and told me he'd be in your room for the time being, to check him out so we could use his room for other guests." My eyes are probably rolling to the back of my head. Leave it to Boston to make a decision like that without bothering to ask or at least relay the memo first. "Honey, you don't look so good." Shit, if I pass out, Boston is going to be upset, and I'll end up in the hospital. His tendency to overreact is like no other, and of course, my medicine is in my room upstairs.

"Yeah, well, don't come any closer with the butt nuggets, please." The thought of her cracking an egg alone has me swallowing. Trying to do the whole mind over matter thing is not helping. "I need to tell you something."

"Oh, oh, oh, oh my gosh. How didn't I know? I'm an idiot. The signs we're all there. You're pregnant!" I watch as she plops the eggs on the counter, none too gently, then her small form bustles around the massive stainless-steel island, and her arms are wrapping around my body, squeezing the life out of me. "My baby is having a baby. I'm going to be a grandma!" Mom's excitement is contagious. I should have known better than to be nervous. It wouldn't matter if my child's father weren't in the picture; this is Mom high on life.

"Isn't this a charming moment." There's a steady clap with each enunciation of the word. I roll my eyes. Fortunately, dear Daddy doesn't see it with my back to him. I'm already a loser in his eyes. Following in his footsteps was never for me. Hell, it's not like he works anyways, living off the rent from the buildings his dad owned before he passed away. Slum Lord, that's exactly what Daddy is, so bad to his tenants it's a wonder they still live there. "How endearing. Our only daughter pregnant without a man in sight, no ring on her finger, and she's still working for her mother when she could be making a name for herself with the Boudreaux name." Still he claps. Mom's body goes ramrod straight. Her hug leaves my body, hand going to mine, squeezing it in our way to be smart. Damn it, where's my pseudo knight in shining armor when I need him?

"I'm not sure why you're here, Noah, but you should leave." One day, Mom will get a restraining order, and if I have any say, it'll be happening today. My hand slides into the pocket of my shorts, pulling my phone out, unsure of his intentions. Him being here this many times, it certainly smells fishy.

"I'm not leaving, Isabelle. We're still married, which means I can be here if I want. Unless you're willing to put this whole divorce issue to rest." And now I'm going to be sick for a different reason entirely.

"Ha, never. Leave now, Noah, or the cops will be here to escort you off my property. And I've got no problem asking for a restraining order." Mom points at the direction of the door. I finally turn around to look at the man who's my father. There is quite literally no love lost.

"You'd never do that. It would disrupt your guests. Isabelle never rocks the boat, or anything for that matter." His voice gets louder. That insinuation is insulting to say the least. I shouldn't be surprised; it's the Noah Boudreaux way.

"What is wrong with you? Are you so spiteful, full of hate, that you have to ruin every single good thing in our lives?" Anger consumes my body, causing my mouth to fly off the handle. Today has been a good day, starting off with celebrating a win in my book by waking up via an orgasm with Boston's fingers thrusting in and out of my wet center, thumb sliding along my clit, making me gasp, all the while feeling his hard and naked cock pressed against my hip. It got better from there, too. No getting sick, talking to my best friend, another person who's happy for me. Of course, the fun sucker Noah Boudreaux would ruin Mom and me celebrating.

"You ungrateful slut. If it weren't for me, you and your mother would be on the street. Now look at you, working at a glorified hotel, pregnant, and where's the father?" Dad's voice rises an octave, no doubt carrying throughout the first floor. With the way LeBlanc Inn is set up, I'm sure it made it through the vents where every single level heard his anger. A slut? Seriously? Me? He's ridiculous. If anyone is a slut, it would be dear old dad here, the male version and the whole reason why Mom is currently in a legal battle that won't stop.

"He's right here," Boston voice carries through the kitchen. "I can't say it's a pleasure to meet." His heat surrounds me, my back to his front. A protective hand slides from my hip, fingers touching my stomach, where our child is safely growing inside me. The worry my father could escalate any and all situation eases with Boston by my side. "It's time you leave, and don't come back. You may know more people in this city than I do, but I've got more money, more time, and a fuck of a lot more power."

I watch as Dad's face turns redder. Virtual steam is come from his ears and nose. Mom had the forethought to move away. When we pulled apart from our hug, she decided to use herself, walking him backwards, putting herself in his line of sight.

"I don't know who you think you are, but you can't talk to me like that. Isabelle is my wife, and Amelie is my daughter. I'm not leaving!" Dad slams his fist down on the countertop near where he stands. I jump back, Boston holding me steady the entire time. I bring my phone up, and unlock it, fingers pressing 9-1-1 without looking. The years texting as a teenager and in college, then working at the Inn, I had to multitask. School, work, social life, you learn how to text without looking. The last thing you want to be doing is walking, looking down at your phone, and run into another person or an object that doesn't bounce back. You'd lose your phone as well as hurt yourself.

"Noah, leave. The last thing anyone wants is for you to make a scene, not for us but for yourself as well," Mom says stoically, maintaining her composure when all I want to do is throw the first available cooking utensil—pot, baking sheet, cast iron skillet, it doesn't matter as long as it hits him in a way that will keep him from running his mouth.

"I told you I am not fucking leaving!" I hit the speaker phone option on my phone.

"9-1-1, what's your emergency?" is blasted throughout the entire kitchen.

"Yes, I'd like to report a trespasser at LeBlanc Inn. We've asked him to leave several times, but he won't. We'd like an officer to escort him off the premises." I just made an enemy. What he doesn't realize is the damn I once gave as a little girl is no longer there. In its place is a woman who will protect her family at all costs.

"This is fucking bullshit. I'm leaving. Amelie, you'll regret this. Isabelle, just you wait until my lawyer gets ahold of your ass. I'll own everything. Every fucking thing. And you, fuck you, coming into my family's place in your expensive clothes. Stupid piece of shit!" My body propels itself forward, breaking away from the hold Boston currently has on me. What will I do once I reach my bastard of a father? Well, I have not one freaking clue. Slap him in the face, knee him in the balls, really, there's no telling. Boston isn't going to let that happen. His hand slides from my hip to my abdomen, and he takes a step back, bringing me with him.

"Calm down, beautiful. A man like that, you don't fight fire with fire. You hit him where it hurts, in his wallet," Boston whispers in my ear. I whip my head over my shoulder, trying to figure out what his game plan involves. He's tight lipped, jaw set, clenching his teeth; it's the look of determination that keeps me from questioning him further.

Finally, Dad decides to leave and gives us his back, slamming through the swinging doors so hard they hit the walls. Mom is startled yet stays standing, a hand to her throat and the weight of the world on her shoulders. "Boston, thank you. I'm not sure how I can ever repay you."

"That's good, because there isn't a need. I'm going to call my attorney. With any luck, he'll be down here tomorrow morning. Amelie, finish the call on the phone. Let them know he left, and you'd like to file a report all the same." He presses a kiss to the side of my head, leaving me reeling yet again. I'm a fish out of water with my mouth opening and closing, attempting to recover from what transpired moments ago.

EIGHTEEN

Boston
_____

"Man, when you need me, you really fucking need me," Sly says into the phone when I call him after what went down.

"You are not wrong. Get whatever you can on Noah Boudreaux and destroy him. This takes precedence over the shit with my parents," I seethe, my eyes still on the two women who are huddled together, talking quietly where Amelie and I were standing before the phone call.

"Holy fuck, that's Amelie's last name. Is this her ex-husband? I kind of need more details, boss." No fucking kidding. I'm going to have to lay it all out now.

"Not her ex-husband. He's Amelie's father. The same piece of shit who tried to sell me the property I wanted. He came in, said a few choice words, and rocked their world. Cops have been

125

called, but who the fuck knows how long it will take for them to actually show up. The call should be in the database. I'll have Ezra hack in to have it on file. He's been fighting Amelie's mom, Isabelle, for nearly a year now, which makes no damn sense. Adultery was involved, so you tell me what you think is really going on. Louisiana isn't a no-fault state in the way of a spouse cheating on the other. The way I see it, Noah Boudreaux has something on the judge, and her lawyer isn't the pit bull mine is." I take a breath and run my hand through my hair, hearing Sly type away on his computer. He's taking notes, always is. You can tell him the most intricate story, and he'll type the cliffs, come up with a strategy and executes it with little to no delay. "Either way, pull whatever strings you have, get this shit as well as the purchase of the building locked and loaded. Then work on the shit stain of my own father. Mom making a play at the same time my dad disowns me publicly speaks volumes now that I think about it."

"I'll grab the transcript from dispatch now. Ezra doesn't need to hack into their database and potentially get caught. I've got someone on my staff who used to work with all those three-letter agencies. She'll be in and out, all doors closed without anyone the wiser. I won't be able to use it in court, but it's something to hold over a head should we need to use that piece of information. As for the other stuff, I'll be down there first thing tomorrow morning. There's a lot I can do from my office, but this I can't. Plus, it'd be nice to see the look on their faces when I slam them with evidence."

"Then I guess I'll see you tomorrow. I'm going to make sure Amelie and Isabelle are alright, then set up a call with the others. Thanks again, Sly," I respond. He's probably got a whole slew of other clients who consume his time. Sylvester taking a day away from the office and court-room means a lot, even if it's coming with a fat-as-fuck bill.

"You got it. Go take care of your girl. I'll text you tomorrow on my way to the Inn."

"Sounds good. Later."

"Later, boss." We hang up. I pocket my phone and walk to where Amelie and her mother are standing. Both look like they've been put through the wringer with small smiles on their faces and color in Amelie's cheeks.

"Everyone okay?" I ask. My hand lingers on Amelie's lower back. Her warmth settles me, her scent intoxicates me, and Christ, her presence grounds me.

"Yeah, Mom was telling me that I need to make our child be a boy. She's spoiled a girl before, and it would be better not to have a girl; they take your beauty, your clothes, and your makeup. Plus, you have to worry about boys sniffing around your teenage daughter." A growl leaves my throat. I've yet to think about the future too far in advance. First things first. Get my house situated, get Amelie moved in, marry her, and then deal with things as they come. But, fuck, now I'm here hoping she has a boy, too, where before I couldn't have cared less.

"Make sure you give me a boy first. The second child can be a girl. I'm going to need as many men around if our daughter is half as beautiful as her mother," I grumble. If we're living down here, my brothers won't be here to help me stand guard either. Shit, I'm going to get an ulcer from worry now.

"Awe, that's so sweet," Isa swoons. Amelie rolls her eyes.

"I'm pretty sure I don't get the choice in the making of a boy or a girl," my woman states.

"You could have twins; they run on you grandmothers' side, who is my mom. Maybe it skipped a generation?" Amelie groans, her head tipping back hitting me in the chest. This woman and her penchant for hitting her head against any object available.

"Hush, take it back. Don't you say it again. Tell her, Boston, two babies at once, oh my gosh, it's like you're asking for me to have saggy baggy's and a stretched vagina." Amelie spins around. "Tell her, tell her right now. You don't understand. If you don't, she'll manifest it, every single day until it happens."

"Sorry, Isabelle, we heard the heartbeat, and there was only one. Maybe next time." I wink for good measure.

"Who said anything about having more children? As far as I'm concerned, you can check into your own room. No one said you can stay with me." Amelie's pointer finger hits my chest. All I can do is laugh. She's a mess. I've never seen this frazzled side of her; it's fucking cute.

"I'm not leaving you. Wherever you are is where I'll always be. And we both know you'll never tell me no." A flush hits her cheeks. Isa hums to herself, giving us this private moment, or semi-private since she knows I've been in her daughter's bed every time I was in New Orleans.

"Whatever. I'm going back to work. All you two do is gang up on me," she throws her attitude around. We both know I'll be fucking it out of her later tonight. I dip my head, lips touching hers, my tongue lapping at her lower lip until she gives me that sweet little gasp I love so much. It's the same one she makes as she comes hard on my cock. Now all I want to do is take her up the three flights of stairs, open her door, and take her against it.

"Boston." I pull back. Taking her in the kitchen probably would be frowned upon. Doesn't mean I'm not tempted.

"Get to work, then meet me upstairs." Her lips are plump from our kiss, eyes sparkling with need and excitement.

"Okay." Her breathless tone is doing nothing to calm my cock down, and when she spins around, showing me an ass I'm going to take, it only makes me that much harder.

NINETEEN

Amelie

I'M ON MY HANDS AND KNEES, NOT A STITCH OF clothing between the two of us. True to Boston's word, he met me upstairs, right on my heels. The door slamming open only to be slammed shut a moment later, my shirt for his, his shoes for mine, then we both worked on taking the rest of our clothes off one another. A rendering of fabric, ripping from its seams in our haste to get our hands on each other was all that mattered. My back was pressed against the wood door, cold to my overstimulated and hot body, Boston's mouth working mine, taking me in a way that shows how much he needs me, his thick cock sliding between my heavily coated lips, allowing him to tease us in a way that had me ripping my mouth away from his, arching my back and lifting a leg to wrap around his waist.

Boston didn't want me like that. No, the man was hell bent on having me where I am right now, ass perched in the air, his hands sliding along the slopes of my curves, and I know exactly why. He wants his cock inside my ass, and while I can't say I'm opposed to it, he's thick, long, and did I say thick? We're still working our way up to that moment. In the meantime, his fingers, toys, and sometimes mouth are all that's happening.

"Oh God, I thought you were deeper before," I groan, fingers clenching the sheets beneath me. The orgasm I was chasing moments ago, before he tossed me in this position, returns at a full throttle. It doesn't seem to take much for an orgasm to be thrown my way. Pregnancy hormones are lighting the fuse faster than you can blow it out. My insides turn to mush, making me annoyed with my body and myself. I wanted this feeling to last. My eyes shutter as he presses his thumb inside my ass, pussy squeezing tightly as I'm tossed into the deep end of the best feeling in the world. And through it all, Boston never falters. My core clenches around his thick and heavy cock at each powerful push of his hips. There's no use in helping him either; he's got me right where he wants me. I'd be a fool to resist. Being stuffed with his dick in my pussy, his thumb in my ass, it's an onslaught of sensations, over-whelming me in the best possible way. I'm dying to feel each spurt of his cum paint my walls.

"Boston," I groan into the pillow. What I'm asking for, I have no idea. All I know is I want more, and I want it to never freaking end.

"Fuck yeah, Amelie. Look at you, taking my cock, sucking my finger into that tight ass of yours. Soon, my cock will be right here,"—he wiggles his thumb—"and you're going to take all of it, a vibrator in your pretty pussy, one tiny wall between where we're both going to enjoy the sensation of each thrust." He slides his thumb in deeper, past the first knuckle. Him talking during sex only amps up my orgasm. I don't need a mirror. I can feel it, imagine it, his cock slick with my wetness, his thumb working in and out in tandem with his thrusts as his fingers grip the side of my ass hard enough that I'll be wearing marks the next day.

He's deeper than before, each of us leading up to the point of trying anal. Boston's size and girth is the one thing holding us back. His hand slides from his grip on my hip to cupping my breast, thumb and finger pulling at my nipple, creating a delicious burn with each twist, pinch, and tug on my sensitive nub.

"More. I need more." He bottoms out inside of me, more of him going faster, more of him going harder, more of him going deeper. All I know is that my brain is going into a fog, full of sensation, the receptors unable to string more than a handful of words together. Boston gets it, though. The hand that was moments ago cupping my breast is now moving upwards, cupping my shoulder, using it for leverage with every plunge of his cock. A wake of goose bumps quivers along my flesh.

"Come on my cock, beautiful. Squeeze the cum out of me. That's what you want, isn't it?" Boston says an inch away from my lips. My exhale is his inhale. The moment is one that will stay locked in my memory bank, the feel of him surrounding my entire being.

"Yes, Boston!" I rip my face away from the covers, crying out with the soul-shattering orgasm, head tipped back, eyes slammed shut, and I feel each punch and swivel of his hips. I don't care that I'm practically screaming the Inn down. The looks I'm sure the employees will give me are a worry for the future. Right now, I'm living in the present. Thank goodness we had the presence of mind to keep my room here as an office for Boston and a bed for me to rest if I get too tired. The bossy man behind me is the only reason I'm even tired, and for reasons like today. A mid-afternoon romp with a nap is exactly what I need.

"Fuck, Amelie, take my cum, my body." I hear his groan, feel it prickle along the outer shell of my ear, knowing it's me who makes him lose control. Jesus, what do they put in these men from New York? Boston allows his body to drop on top of me, careful of how much of his weight he gives me.

"I think you've fucked my cock to death, Amelie." He pulls out and rolls onto his back, bringing me closer until I'm practically on top of him. A mess oozes from between my legs, but neither of us cares.

"Give him ten minutes, and he'll be ready for more," I say before he takes my mouth with his, dominating the kiss much like he dominated my orgasm.

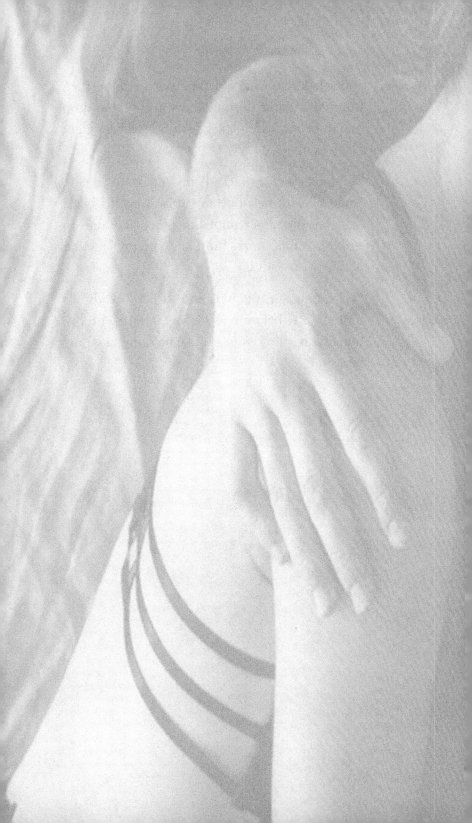

TWENTY

Amelie

"ARE YOU FEELING OKAY?" BOSTON ASKS ME THE next day. I'm on my stomach, still naked from the night before where he had no problem wearing me out, keeping the wolves at bay by wringing my body with a copious amount of orgasms. It worked, too. The tips of his fingers trail up and down my back in zig zags, circles, all kinds of different patterns, it doesn't matter. All I know is that it feels amazing. I grouse when he stops the movement, and he picks it back up almost instantly.

"I am. Mom isn't cooking eggs, thank goodness, and I'm in your arms. The only niggle in the back of my mind is you're having to wade into my pile of shit, taking care of an issue that you were thrust in. I really hate that part." Today, we're supposed to meet with Sylvester, Boston's friend and attorney, for multiple reasons—my father, Mom's divorce, the building he's purchasing, and then because Boston is an overachiever, he wants to go take a look at furniture for his new place. A place where Boston has stated I'm moving into. I ignored him. The demanding fool attempted to withhold an orgasm from me while insisting that's where I'll be. I held my own. He might have pulled out, but it didn't last for long. His mouth attached to my clit, my hands clamping down the back of his head, then I was coming on one long moan. Needless to say, no more talking happened.

"That's good. I don't want you worrying. The pregnancy book said an expectant mother shouldn't have a lot of stress in her life. It causes things like an increase in high blood pressure; pre-eclampsia could happen." I tip my head toward his, rolling my eyes the entire time. I'm going to kill his friend Parker for overnighting that damn thing. Literally, the next time I'm near a lighter, I'm going to set it on fire.

"I'm fine. Women have been carrying babies for centuries, and I'm sure they've had way more stress than I've experienced." Okay, maybe not quite as much, but I'm willing to bet it's right along the same playing field. At least I've got a massive support system, minus a father, who's a raging prick.

"Still, it's my job to take care of you, and it's one I want to do, take away any stress I can, including helping your mother. She should be able to walk around carefree, work at the Inn without being worried her husband is going to barge his way inside and strong-arm her. I've got the money and the power. What good is it if I don't use it in a way that's beneficial to the woman I love?" Boston Wescott has stunned me silent. My mouth is opening and closing, like a fish out of water. The man who tossed the four-letter word out uses his the side of his pointer finger and thumb to close it. "You heard me right, Amelie. I'm well aware we've got a few hurdles to jump through—your father, my family, a baby that I'll give my life for with no questions asked." My breath is lodged in my throat, eyes filling with tears, unable to control my damn emotions. Everything Boston said, it's exactly what I want—him, our child, my mom to be okay. Fuck the rest, whatever happens.

"I love you, Boston. I think I have all along. You may have left me, and that still hurts at times, but I know why you did it, even understand it a bit, but if you ever do that again, I will fly to New York or wherever your ass is and kick you in the balls, no matter the fact we will be having more than one child together." He must like what I said. My naked body is no longer pressed against his; I'm flat on my back, his hands on my wrists, holding them hostage above my head.

The look in the father of our child's eyes is one of pure devotion.

"Amelie, as God as my witness, with every depth of my fucking being, I am not leaving without you ever again. I screwed up, believing I was trying to protect you from my own father and his personal vendetta against me and Four Brothers. I should have known better, abandoning you with a different type of wolf. I'm sorry I almost missed out on this, and not just my cock being in its happy place. But I mean the doctor's visit, hearing our baby for the first time. Fuck, I'd have never forgiven myself. I watched yesterday as you stood your ground against Noah, and, beautiful, I have no doubt in my mind that when it comes to Governor Wescott you can hold your own." He wedges his body closer to mine. The muscles in his arms ripple, causing me to lick my lips. A different kind of emotion is taking over. One that's filled with nothing but lust, desire, and love.

"You're forgiven, though I'll take more apologies in the form of orgasms. Plus, what you're doing for my mom, it's unbelievable, and I'm so incredibly thankful." He lowers his body further. My eyes slide away from his fiery orbs, tracing the slope of each perfectly sculpted muscle of his chest and abdomen, watching his heavy cock bob once then twice.

"Good, now that we have shit settled, it's time for me to start on the first of many orgasms to come." I'm silenced once again with his lips and tongue. My legs wrap around his waist, and with one movement, Boston is seated deep inside me, making me realize that maybe I forgave him too fast. The rewarded orgasms are pretty freaking spectacular.

TWENTY-ONE

Boston

"BINGO," SYLVESTER SAYS LATER IN THE DAY. Amelie is currently bustling back and forth between the kitchen and the front concierge area. One of the Inn's employees called in sick, some kind of stomach bug. The only thing that's keeping me calm and not lashing out is that my eyes are on her at all times. Our slow and easy morning turned into running one errand after another, starting with meeting Sly at the office building, which is currently under contract; the only thing we're waiting on is for the owner to sign the papers, all-cash offer, no contingencies or inspections were necessary. The building needs a lot of work, not enough for it to be a complete tear-down, but it will need work from the inside out. As much as I'd like to beautify the outside, helping restore another piece of history in the area, too much could go wrong, like windows being blown out by the demo crew, brickwork shaking from jackhammering to replace the plumbing, and that's only the half of it. Sylvester whistling when he saw the shape of the place was all too telling. The same couldn't be said for Amelie. There were stars in her eyes as she spilled out ideas to preserve what could be salvaged, going so far as to pull up pictures of how the building once stood in its glory.

"You've got something, don't you?" I look up from my own work of starting a spreadsheet and proposal for Four Brothers. Even if they have no problem with me branching out, I want it fucking official and them to sign off on it. Plus, each of us brings something different to the table; they may notice something I missed, or vice versa.

"Fuck, yes, do I ever." He turns his laptop around, showing me a multitude of listings on the MLS website. He must notice my confusion. "I've tracked back each owner, compared them to the listing agent, then I did the same for the agent. Found a massive discrepancy after my IT tech said the real estate company was an umbrella company." Four Brothers knows all about that, using our own when shit went down with Ezra's woman, Millie.

"You're shitting me. How did I not notice that this same agency has all of these listings?" I ask him.

"Because all of these were added recently. When you looked at Isabelle's parents' building, there were only a few under this agency. Now there are more than ten, all bunched together. Someone was thinking they're slick. Not as slick as my tech. I don't know how Noah Boudreaux can afford this since he's claiming he's destitute with his financial affidavit. He owns the umbrella company. What he doesn't own is all these houses. A quick look at the property appraiser's website tells me everything I need. He's going down, and I've barely scratched the surface." There's a gleam in his eyes. This is the shit he lives for, dissecting a case to put it all back together.

"Does that mean he's selling property he doesn't own, lying to a judge, his attorney either being none the wiser or playing right along with him? Holy fuck, man. Isabelle has been trying to divorce this asshat for nearly nine months. Noah has no idea who he's fucking with." One worry is off my shoulders. The same can't be said for the rest. Two steps forward and one step back has been the name of the game for a month now.

"I'm willing to bet you a million dollars his attorney is part owner in the umbrella company and that the judge is bought and paid for, too." I sit back in my chair, running my hand down my face. Son of a bitch. This is going to destroy Amelie, to hear about your father swindling not only your mom but also other innocent people, trying to take it so far that Isabelle would have to pay him some kind of compensation. It's an entirely fucked-up situation.

"What's the next step? I mean, back home, we'd bust this shit right open, leak it to the press, and let them have a hay day with it." So much for protecting Amelie from added stress. She's going to carry this until the bitter end, and if Sly can't figure out how to make Boudreaux pay back all the money he's taken from innocent bystanders, well, she'll really lose her shit.

"I'm going to do some digging on his attorney and judge, then do the same as we would in New York. Which sucks for you. I'm assuming you'll be with Isabelle and Amelie every step of the way. You'll be putting everyone, including yourself, on your father's radar. I've yet to dig deep into what Mrs. Wescott talked about. The more I think on the topic, the leerier I am about the situation."

"I'll be with her. I'm not letting her or Isabelle's ass swing in the wind without some kind of protection. It wouldn't be a bad idea to hire some security. Neither of them are going to close the Inn, and they damn sure aren't going to stop going on with their day." I start going through other variables. Amelie can hold her own should she have to deal with my parents; it's the media shit storm that can be fucking brutal.

"We'll get that taken care of well before the case breaks." Sly nods, thinking the same as me.

"As for my family, it might not be a bad idea to get ahead of whatever they're scheming, there is no doubt in my mind, mom will do whatever it is to make sure she's sitting in the green. Even if it's helping dear old dad out, no matter how many times he bangs his secretary. Wescott is the money chain, and she's there to ride the coat-tails." The more I replay the conversation with Sly, the less optimistic I am that my mother is doing anything out of the goodness of her black soul.

"Already ahead of you. The Wescott's are proving a bit more difficult to tap into without leaving any footprints. By the time we bring this to the press, I'll have that lined up as well."

"Shit, man, I owe you a kidney. The house, the building, Isabelle's situation, and my family. I'm scared to see the bill," I joke with him.

"You can win it back at a game of poker. Besides, everyone knows this is chump change for the both of us. It's the thrill of the chase, you for money, me for winning a case." On that we can agree.

"Alright, I'm taking a break. It's time to find my woman and get her off her feet." I get out of my seat. She's yet to come into the kitchen during this conversation, meaning I haven't seen her for nearly as long.

"Good luck. She's going to bust your balls." He turns back to his work, and I walk out of the kitchen. The only thing I care about is making sure Amelie is okay. The other shit can fall where it lands.

TWENTY-TWO

Amelie

"I'M NOT SURPRISED, MOM, AND YOU REALLY can't be either." Sylvester and Boston sat us both down to give us the news about what my father has been doing. Mom has tears in her eyes, not for herself, for others. Me, I'm fighting mad, ready to hit Dad below the belt, preferably in a pair of Doc Marten boots between the legs.

"It doesn't make it any easier to hear." She's right. Of course, she is. My mother always has been.

"With everything I have, the attempt to sell your property, the trespassing, a cop never coming out to take your statement, the way he was selling property without consent, his lawyer paying off the judge. I don't think you'll have a problem receiving the divorce you deserve. Boston will tell you everything else. This is going to be a media sensation. The Inn will no doubt be inundated with calls, press, and people wanting to book a vacation after hearing what you've been through," Sylvester states calmly. Boston is sitting next to me, his arm dangling behind my back along the chair. His other is holding my hand, fingers entwined, squeezing ours together every now and then.

"Won't they be disgusted with me? What if everyone believes I knew about what Noah was doing?" Mom asks, hyperaware of the fallout.

"That won't happen. We've got ahold of the situation before it even happens. Sylvester will make a statement on your behalf, and we'll go from there. In the meantime, we're going to stay at the Inn, let it blow over before moving into my home." I roll my eyes at his obnoxious state- ment. No one agreed to me leaving the Inn to live with Boston, especially the person being me. This thick-headed man is out to undermine me, swoop in, and while he's already the hero in everyone's eyes, including mine, telling me I'm moving in without asking me, oh, I'm going to make him sweat.

"Oh, you're moving? I think this is a fabulous idea. I've been telling Amelie for years now, the Inn has been my dream, but it doesn't have to be hers," Mom inserts. I totally knew she'd be gung-ho with Boston and his big mouth.

"It's a good thing that it's also my dream. The only reason grandaddy's building is sitting empty right now is because of the circumstances of your divorce, which will be done and over soon, it seems." We always wanted to have both the LeBlanc buildings open, flourishing, and bringing in money along with tourists.

"Honey, you have to know you're going to have your hands full by the end of the year. Sure, right now, you're only battling morning sickness with certain smells. What are you going to do when the birth of my grandchild is looming? I don't think it's a good idea to even contemplate starting something of that magnitude. Boston, will you help me out?" Oh, brother, here we go. I guess I'll be calling Eden soon to complain to her, not that she'll agree with me. One thing about the people in my life who love me, they also protect me to an extreme it's almost suffocating.

"Amelie, you want to start restoring it while you're pregnant, I'll get a crew on it, but you absolutely are running yourself ragged, opening up a new Inn when you're already dead on your feet every night here, and it's nothing compared to having an established business. You know what stress does to a mother." I swear to all that is holy I'm going to give Boston something to stress about with my hands around his throat.

"I see this is getting us nowhere. I know when I'm losing an uphill battle. Sylvester, thank you for all your help. Boston, I'm going back to work. Yes, I'd like for the other potential LeBlanc to be restored as long as Mom is okay with that. I can see where you're both coming from; I'm also not an invalid. Now, I'm going back to work." I stand up from my chair. Boston is smirking. He got his way. He and my mother are in cahoots with one another, I swear.

"You're welcome, Amelie. I'll make sure everything goes smoothly for your mom and the court hearing, should it even go that far. I have a feeling with the case I present, it'll be settled, and then Noah, his attorney, and the presiding judge will be more than likely prosecuted federally, meaning my job may be done in the next week or so." Sylvester is a man of action, not so much words, which is fine with me. He can also be a little intimidating, and from what Boston told me, the only soft spot he has is for his secretary. There's some juicy gossip no one is talking about. Maybe when we eventually go to Boston's hometown, meet his brothers and their women, I can get the tea.

"Even better. Mom, I'll manage the front until the new shift comes on. Boston, I'll see you later." Boston's hand encompasses mine, pulling me down until his mouth is at my ear. My body lights up, and while part of me wants to blame the pregnancy-induced hormones, I can't. It's Boston. It's always Boston.

"Keep your ass planted on the barstool I placed behind the desk. I come out and see you standing, your ass is going to feel the delicious sting of my palm, beautiful," he whispers his threat in my ear. My libido soars, and I already know I'm going to defy him. Reaping the rewards in the form of another spectacular orgasm definitely has its appeal.

TWENTY-THREE

Amelie

ONE MONTH LATER

"THAT WAS NOT in the *What to Expect* book."
Boston acts like he's the one on the table, legs
spread, feet settling in stirrups while a look-alike
of a dildo is sliding inside his vagina, condom
included. Nope, he's sitting in the chair, much
like last month, in slacks and a button-down
shirt, ever the wealthy businessman. Unlike the
state of my undress, a gown wrapped around
my body and sheet over my lap as we wait for
the ultrasound tech to come back in.

"I'm going to light that book on fire. That, or
I'm going to throw it at your head. Never in my
life did I think Boston Wescott would be the one
who is proverbially shivering in his boots over an

ultrasound or any other little nuance," I tell him. Boston and that stupid book, bless Parker's wife if she's dealing with him like I am Boston and boy am I going to give her all the ammunition I can for her to use when she's pregnant and Parker suddenly starts acting like Boston.

"Always threatening bodily harm, then changing your tune the moment my mouth, hands, or cock come out to play." I did the unthinkable—I gave in, entirely too easily. There wasn't enough room for Boston to stay in my room at the Inn and work there as well. His building is currently in the beginning stages of renovations and will take way too long for him to continue working at a small table. So, since the thought of not sleeping with Boston every night wasn't what I wanted, nor did he, I moved out of the Inn. With that came on an off-switch I had no idea my body needed.

"Boston, sshh!" Thankfully, we're saved from any more conversation when the ultrasound tech knocks on the door.

"Are you ready to see your baby?" she asks cheerily. In the past month, life has literally been smooth sailing, almost to the point that you know the other shoe is going to land in a pile of shit, or however that stupid saying goes.

"Yes, so much," I tell her, watching as she sits down on the stool.

"We won't be able to find out the sex today, will we?" Boston asks. I close my eyes as I lie back on the table, scooting down until my ass is almost hanging off the ledge. He knows very well we won't be able to determine the sex yet. His stupid book gives him a play-by-play, and while he's already itching to ask for the bloodwork in order to know the sex of our child, I'd rather wait. I'm not above getting my own way either.

"No, that would be at your next ultrasound appointment. Mom, this is going to be cold, I'm sorry." She lubes up the probe. Boston grunts. The thought of a toy sliding inside me is not his idea of fun. Mine either, buddy. It's not like I'm getting an ounce of sexual enjoyment out of this.

"That's okay. It'll be worth it. Boston, come hold my hand?" Maybe keeping him away from my legs and up by my head will calm his attitude down; all hopes of him staying seated were thrown out the window.

"I'm going to do a few measurements before we'll get to the fun parts." The room is quiet. Boston's eyes are focused on the screen, squinting at the tiny plum-sized baby. Another one of his doings was putting an app on each of our phones, giving us a weekly reminder on the development, size, and what to expect, a version of that damn book he keeps on the coffee table in the living room. Believe me, I've tried to hide it, but he figures out where it is instantly, almost like he has eyes in the back of his head or cameras in the house, which I know he doesn't. I even threw it in the trash can. He dug it out, used sanitizing wipes, and pretended I wasn't standing there with my hands on my hips while trying not to laugh at his antics. I was ready to relentlessly tease him, even though I know Boston is coming from a good place, making sure he's nothing like his father. All of those thoughts ended when he walked up to me, kissed me until I breathless before carrying on with his reading material.

"Are you okay?" he asks, his all-time favorite question since I told him about my pregnancy. I'm sure he feels the dampness from my hand. This is our first ultrasound. I worried myself sick to mom earlier today, thinking about everything that could go wrong, feeling like life is going way too easy lately for there not to be an issue of some sort.

"Not sure." I shrug my shoulders, my eyes moving back to the screen. I wait on abated breath for the tech to finish up, ready to ask her questions like Boston does.

"Alright, everything looks good. Your baby is growing right on schedule. If anything, he or she might be a tad bigger in the growth scale. Were either of you big babies?" she asks.

"I was average, around seven pounds," I tell her.

"I'm not sure, to tell the truth." Another facet of Boston's family unfolds. I wouldn't put it past his parents not to have a baby book of him. He may have been born into the life of wealth, but the love he missed out on could never take its place in money.

"Ready to hear the heartbeat?" I nod vigorously. The news she gave us loosened the muscles around my heart, an ache so deep in my chest, I had no idea it was possible to love something so much without having them in your hands.

"Yes, please," Boston tells her the words I'm unable to. Emotion clogs my throat every time we're at the doctor's office, which makes talking difficult. At least now my morning sickness is pretty much gone, though eggs still turn me off something fierce—the smell, the runny yolk—so much so that Mom now has me come into the Inn after brunch is through, meaning my hours have been cut drastically. I wouldn't be surprised if Boston had something to do with that, too.

The *woosh, woosh, woosh* echoes through the room for the second time since we found out I was pregnant. We listen for as long as we can while she goes through the rest of the ultrasound, showing us where the hands and feet are forming, the umbilical cord. When it's over, Boston somehow manages to finagle her out of so many pictures I'm sure there's enough for our whole fridge along with Mom's. I don't say anything, because seeing the man you love in full dad mode hits you right in the feels.

TWENTY-FOUR

Boston

"Today is cause for a celebration. It's not every day I get to see a picture of my grandbaby. And would you look at this!" Isabelle turns on the television in the kitchen, blaring it louder than I thought she would since at one point, Isa wanted to keep this completely under wraps. It seems those days are over with judging by the television reporting the news. A prominent member of a local news station is currently talking. My hold on Amelie tightens, bringing her to my front, hand sliding to her lower abdomen, where our child is nestled inside. I'm in constant worry that between my shit storm of a family and hers, it will do something to take the most precious thing away from us.

"I'm Amanda Walker, reporting from the New Orleans Police Department, where an update is imminent. It appears Noah Boudreaux along

with his attorney, Martin Strong, and Judge
Maroon have been escorted from three different
police cars. What we're hearing is that these
three men are being arrested for supposedly a
slew of charges. Noah Boudreaux, from what
we're hearing, is the leader of this group, finding
abandoned buildings and selling them without
the owners' consent. His attorney, Martin
Strong, did the paperwork and created an
umbrella corporation to funnel the funding into
an offshore account, where Judge Maroon is
accused of signing off on undisclosed documents." Amelie's hands clap together, probably
in excitement. The past month, Sly has been
doing his due diligence, working behind the
scenes making sure that when he handed over
the evidence, it wasn't to a crooked district attorney. It was hard to fathom that there could
potentially be so many, but I saw what a judge
was willing to sweep under the rug, trying to get
Isabelle to pay spousal support when Noah had
more than enough from him stealing from
anyone he could.

"I mean, I know the divorce won't be final, but
if he's in jail, he can't bother us, none of us. I'm
literally free, for the first time since this whole
debacle started." Isa is twirling around in the
kitchen, floating on the high on life she deserves.
Amelie is in my arms, a smile plastered on her
face as she watches her mom on cloud nine.

"I'm happy for you, Mom." She pulls out of my arms and moves toward Isabelle. The two of them hug while employees walk in and out of the kitchen to see the news and gather around, waiting their turn to celebrate no longer seeing Noah Boudreaux at the end. My phone vibrating in my pocket pulls my eyes away from the woman who owns me.

"Hello." Sylvester's name flashes on the display.

"Brother, I know you probably got the news already. I wish it were me there to deliver it face to face to Isabelle. Sadly, I've got a case that's busting my balls."

"Watching my woman and her mom celebrate right now. I've never seen Amelie happier besides when we saw our baby today. Fuck, that was amazing. A case is kicking your ass, or your secretary is making you sweat?" I prod, trying to get to the truth. He'd do the same to me. Hell, he did not long ago, when I was a miserable shit, brooding and closed off, working more than my usual trying to keep any and all heat away from Amelie while getting things together to bring Four Brothers to New Orleans. It all worked out in the end. Not sure how I managed it, yet I did.

"A bit of both. She's on some tangent about needing to save the whales and dolphins, wants me to take on philanthropic work. I don't have the heart to tell her that for every company you take down for illegally killing wildlife, four more appear. Add on the other cases, plus digging around in your parents' accounts without leaving a trace, and I need a damn vacation." I chuckle. It's hard not to. Sylvester Sterling's dick is all in knots over a woman who's nearly a foot shorter than him, younger by nearly fifteen years, and the best part about it is, she doesn't see that Sly is panting for her like a dog in heat.

"From the bill Four Brothers paid this morning, I'd say you can buy a small island, spend a month there, and still have plenty of money."

"And what would I do with my secretary? Leave her to the fucking sharks in this building? Don't answer that. I don't want to hear your opinion. Congratulations, man, I'm happy for you." Sly knows his secretary is who he wants; it's coming to terms with it more than anything.

"I appreciate it. You going to be around this weekend?" I ask. Parker and I spoke earlier today. Papers need to be signed. I want Amelie to meet the rest of my brothers, and a weekend away isn't a bad idea either.

"Yep. You coming home?" I don't think of New York as home anymore. The only home I'll ever need isn't a place; it's a person.

"We are. I'll let you know the details as soon as I've got them laid out." We hang up. There's another way I'm ready to celebrate, and it's with Amelie, any way I can have her.

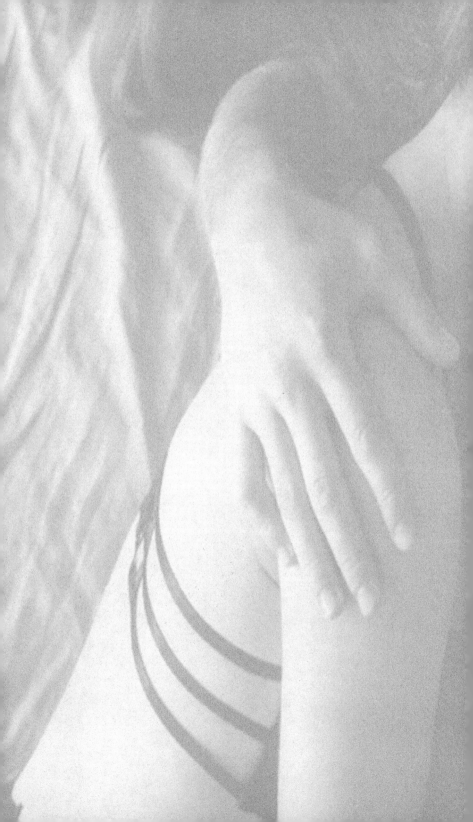

TWENTY-FIVE

Amelie

I'M STANDING IN BOSTON'S NEW YORK brownstone a few days after the news came out. Mom is happier than ever, as she should be, though there's still a lot left up in the air. Only time will tell what's going to happen. For now, Dad is behind bars, as is his attorney. The judge was somehow released on bond. Make it make sense. So, when Boston suggested I go along with him on a work trip to New York City, it was hard to say no. Mom practically shoved me out the door. For someone who says she loves me, she sure doesn't want me around as much anymore. All Boston's doing, I'm sure. His mission to drive me up the wall and smother me to no end can get annoying even if it's coming from a good place. Still, I came willingly, wanting to get away from the press. Today is the day. Boston and I are hosting a lunch of sorts, with all of them, and I do mean every last one of his friends who are thicker than any blood could possibly be. Parker and his wife, Nessa. Ezra and Millie; I'm unsure if they're married or engaged. Don't judge me. There's four of them and one of me, well, five if you count Sylvester, who is single yet taken, so says Boston. And Theo, who no one knows whether he's dating or not. All five of them live within walking distance. A part of me feels bad that Boston has given up a lot of his roots to settle in New Orleans, which has me coming up with a scheme of my own.

My second trimester is treating me amazingly. My energy levels are back, my libido is more insatiable, though I have no idea how that was even possible. I only know that it is, and if Boston doesn't get his ass downstairs soon, I'll be meeting them on my own. The game plan is to meet up here, let the guys go over a few things for work, then we'll walk to a restaurant nearby. The grumble in my stomach is yelling at me to eat a snack. No problem. Now that my morning sickness is out of the way, my appetite is back in full force. I take out the tray with assorted cheeses, crackers, and salami, my favorite these days. Boston did most of it since he had it prepared as well as the fridge stocked before we even walked through the doors.

"Hmmm," I moan, taking my first bite, not even bothering to make a plate or wait until the tray is on the counter. I lift the saran wrap and sneak my fingers inside for the salami and mozzarella. Crackers be damned. I just need something now. Boston's child demands food on the regular, and if he or she doesn't get it, well, I'm left hungry, angry, and with a killer headache. This pregnancy hasn't been smooth sailing like some others I know, but I'm alright with it. I'm better than most, and I'm still able to get up, work, and get on with my daily tasks. I finish that bite, this time with more patience. I make another little sandwich with crackers, leaning over the sink because of the crumbs that will to no doubt fall when I bite into the goodness.

"Amelie, will you grab the door? I'll be right down," Boston interrupts my moment with food. How does he know anyone is at the door? I didn't hear a doorbell. I grumble and take the last bite, stuffing it in my mouth as I dust off the crumbs from my hands and off the sink, then do the same to my face as I make my way to the front door. I should be annoyed that I'm meeting all his friends face to face for the first time without him. The truth of the matter is, I'm not. I've met Sylvester, talked to the others a handful of times, and Boston has a relationship with them that's so close I feel like we've already met.

"Hey, guys," I say with a smile on my face after making my way to the massive wood door, unlocking the deadbolt and lock on the knob, twisting it, and flinging the door open. Only to stand in front of who I know as Governor Wescott. A sense of déjà vu hits me. Here is another irate-looking man. Oh, joy. Lucky freaking me.

"Where's Boston?" he demands. I cross my arms over my breasts, hip cocked out, foot holding the back of the door open, letting him know that he will not be let in. Over my dead fucking body. Boston protected me. Now it's my turn to protect the man I love more than myself.

"He's busy." We're in a deadlock of who will blink first. He may be a wealthy politician, but I've dealt with far worse. My own father was the definition of crooked, and while I don't know the entire story of why the man in front of me is a vile piece of shit, I'm knowledgeable in the fact that Boston has a relationship with most anyone. Even if he doesn't know you, he's at least cordial.

"Make him unbusy. Are you the slut of the week for my son? I can see he has good taste. Nice tits, curves, and a mouth made for sucking cock." How I remain stoic, unlike my normal self that would unleash a slew of words right back in his face, along with a swift kick in the tiny balls he so clearly sports, is a damn miracle. I also know his type. He thrives on making people tick. Belittling them with each word is how he works. Too bad I had my own version of hell in the form of a father. Governor Wescott isn't anything to write home about. A bully in his own respect, throwing out words to make you feel worse about yourself.

"Like I said, he's busy. I'll let him know you stopped by." My arms drop from my chest. He must see that I'm going to close the door, because as I go to shut it, his foot is at the ready, pushing it back open so hard that I'm almost knocked on my ass. Except it doesn't happen. Boston is at my back, cushioning my blow, and judging by the growl coming from him, I'm going to have to diffuse this situation, fast.

"Governor Wescott, I do believe you're trespassing." My eyes move downward, seeing he is certainly standing within the foyer of Boston's house. "I'd suggest you leave. Now," Boston grounds out. The vibration from his chest hits my back.

"I paid for this place. I'll damn well stay here with your little two-bit whore if I want to!" Jesus, can't anyone come back with something original? This is getting tiring. Slut, whore, it's all the same for men who think they're better than anyone else, especially when it's them who are those names.

"Leave now." Boston starts to move me out of his way when we're saved by the miracles of all miracles. Sylvester is front and center, followed by Parker, Ezra, Theo, Nessa, and Millie in the background, probably because their men knew

Boston wouldn't leave his door open to invite the man who makes everyone's life a living hell.

"Governor Wescott, so nice of you to drop by my client's home, which he purchased with his own money. You wouldn't happen to know about his inheritance that's suddenly missing, would you?" Boston's body locks up behind me. I let out a small squeak. Holy shit. Surely, the governor wouldn't take money that wasn't his, right?

"I have no idea what you're talking about." Wescott tries to brush it off, turning around to face Sylvester. I wish he'd take a long walk off a short bridge.

"I bet. It was good to see you, Wescott. I'm sure we'll be seeing more of you, too." Sly shrugs his shoulders and takes a step closer until Boston's father has no other choice but to walk by, and with the space Sylvester is taking up, it's Wescott who has to squeeze by.

"You're on my radar, Sterling. Watch your back. Boston, I suggest you leave New York, take your trollop with you, and never return." Well, then, I'll give him an A for effort. Can't say that's been used on me in the past month or so. These men are something else.

"I do believe you just made a threat. Probably not your wisest move, with witnesses are all around. The governor running for presidency and all," Sly inserts. Wescott must get the memo. His mouth is firmly shut. He should probably see about gluing his lips together permanently. Everyone watches as he walks away.

"Well, that was interesting. I guess both our fathers are rays of sunshine on a cloudy day," I joke to lighten the mood.

"Always a pleasure, Amelie," Sly says.

"We won't have to deal with either of them much longer, beautiful," Boston whispers along the shell of my ear. "Amelie, meet everyone. Everyone, Amelie, the mother of my child and my fiancée." This time, it's me spinning around. No way did he just tell me I'm going to marry him.

"Boston!" A chorus of laughs and awes sound behind me as I watch as he drops to one knee, ring in hand.

"This isn't how I was planning to ask you to marry me, but now is the best time. My family is with us. They know how much we love one another. Amelie, marry me." It's still not a question, more of a statement. I don't care. I'm already nodding, eyes full of tears, and he's back on his feet, arms around my body, hugging me while picking me up, lips locked with mine, celebrating while our friends do the same surrounding us.

TWENTY-SIX

Boston

"You okay after what went down?" Parker asks from across the table. They came inside, we talked a bit, did our introductions, then Amelie demanded real food. The snack tray I had put together before we landed wasn't cutting it, and I know the mother of my child. It was time for food, carbs preferably.

"I am. More pissed that every male thinks it's okay to call a woman a demoralizing name. Twice now I've had to keep my hands to myself. It's fucking annoying." Noah would have spun it in a way in order to rip money off me. My father would slander the hell out of me and bring Four Brothers into the mix. No one would win.

"You're doing well. Let Sly take care of the rest. It's better to stay under the radar, like we did not long ago," Ezra says.

"If anyone is going to kick that cocksucker's ass, it's going to be me. I've got not one single thing to lose." Theo, our usual voice of reason, is itching for a fight. Either that or he needs to get laid.

"I've got it under control. You four jackasses keep your panties out of a twist. My office is working on something. Once we have a solid game plan, we'll meet up." Sylvester states.

"We're not leaving until Monday, you all want to get together tomorrow, meet at the gym," I tell them.

"Nessa is working tomorrow." Parker isn't one to leave the house or office unless Vanessa is at work or she drags him out from his cave.

"That will work. Millie does account shit first thing in the morning, so make it early." Ezra is much like Parker and me, driving her to the coffee shop, making sure she's safely inside and an employee is there with her.

"I'll be there," Theo rounds out. We each start our own conversations. Sylvester getting my attention.

"Congrats, brother, you deserve it," he tells me as the waiter and waitress set down the bowls of salads, baskets of bread sticks, and trays of pizza. The restaurant was the women's choice. They each wanted something different, but they finally came up with a plan and decided on a little Italian pizzeria down the street from our homes. The food is good, the service is impeccable, and most importantly, there isn't a wait.

"Thanks." Amelie fits right in, not that I had any doubt she would. "And thank you for what you did back there."

"Anyone would have done it. I wanted to see him shake in his boots, secretly hoping he'd give something away. Which he did. I watched him leave, no words to be spoken, meaning he's being watched," Sly replies.

"Well, by doing that, you're on his radar now. You've got a secretary, one who won't be able to handle a guy like that. The governor doesn't go after one person; he takes the people you care about down first, ripping them apart little by little. The only time I'll have to deal with dear old Dad is when I'm in New York, which won't be very much, every other month for a quick trip, and he damn sure wouldn't leave the state of New York unless it's to campaign for presidency."

"I've got it covered, even if I need to sequester her away and out of the office. Don't you worry about me. I knew the can of worms I was opening when I held a meeting with your mom. Finding out the other stuff along the way sealed the deal." Sylvester knows what he's doing. I'm still going to warn him. This is my shit he's stepping in.

"If you're sure." Amelie is sitting with Nessa and Millie, talking a mile a minute. The yawn she keeps hiding behind the palm of her hand leads me to believe she's holding out on my behalf.

"I'm positive. Stay sharp all the same."

"Always. I'm going to take my fiancée home. See you tomorrow. I'd like to know more about that little bombshell you dropped at my place." Talking about it in public would be stupid, too many prying eyes and ears willing to do anything to run a story.

"Sounds good. Later, brother." I stand up and make my way around the table until I get to Amelie. My hand is out. She takes it with a mischievous smile written on her face. Fuck yeah, she might have been yawning, but that twinkle in her eyes tells me all I need to. My fiancée is ready to start the real celebration, and I'm more than ready.

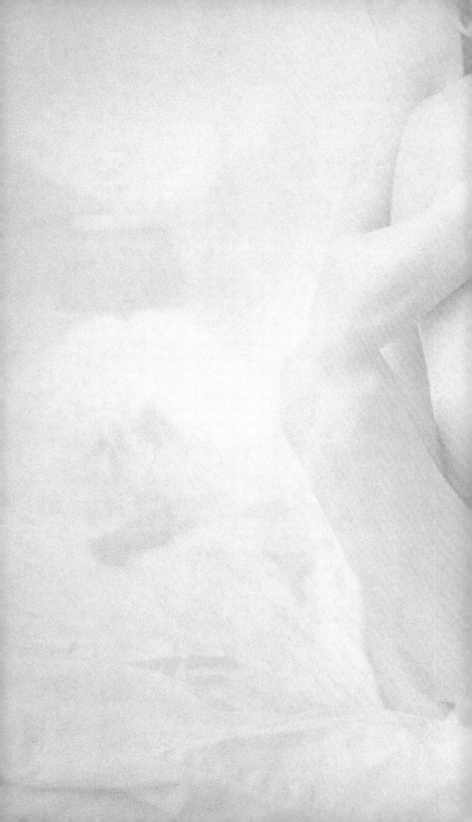

Epilogue

Boston

SIX MONTHS LATER

"YOU CAN DO THIS, Amelie. A few more pushes, and our baby will be in your arms." I see the determination written on her face. I also see the tiredness. She's been pushing for nearly an hour now, and it's taking its toll. Amelie is dead set on giving birth vaginally, not for any other reason than because if she has to have a cesarean section, she'll be down longer, which means less time to put what she calls the final touches on LeBlanc Inn part deux. Fuck that. It's stupid, if you ask me. She's got employees

187

who can help. Not only that, Isabelle would gladly step in.

"I'm going to kill you for knocking me up, Boston Wescott!" The grip on my hand tightens. Taking her anger out on me works.

"One more push, Amelie, then we'll have the head out. You can do this," her doctor says between her legs. Her feet are propped in stirrups. Amelie made me promise I'd stay close to her head, or I'd never be between her legs again. I call bullshit, but rocking the boat I was not.

"You got this, beautiful. A few more minutes, and we'll finally know the sex of our baby." We were like water and oil when it came to finding out if we were expecting a boy or a girl. She wanted it to be a surprise, whereas I wanted to know right away, trying to push a blood test in order to find out as soon as humanly possible. Amelie wasn't having that. A few rounds of bickering back and forth, and she won. There was no reason for me to push her into some kind of stress-induced issue, but the gloating that came from her is one I'm still living with months later.

"I can do this. I can. I know I can," my fiancée tells herself out loud, pushing with all her might. She's right. The woman is a force to be reckoned with. Strong and determined, not afraid to fight battles that aren't hers to begin with.

"The head is out. One last push, and your baby will be here." My mind goes blank. Our child will finally be here. The trials, the tribulations, the hurt I put Amelie through, and she prevailed through it all, forgiving me when she shouldn't have, but fuck am I thankful she did all the same.

"You're there, Amelie. So close, beautiful, so damn close." Gone is the anger. In its place is awe as we hear the first sign of our baby, the loud wail. One last push, and then the doctor is holding our child. I kiss Amelie's lips; tears are streaming down her cheeks.

"A girl. We have a beautiful baby girl." Outside the doors, sitting in the waiting room, are Amelie's mom, her best friend, Eden, and her husband, Kavanaugh, my brothers, and their significant others, waiting to hear how mom and baby are doing. Parker, Ezra, Theo, and Sly are more or less waiting to know how I'm going to handle having a little girl who I know will look exactly like her mother. I'm going to be fucked, fucked, fucked.

I watch as they place her on Amelie's chest. She pulls the gown down so they're skin to skin. "Boston, look at our baby. We have a girl."

"She's beautiful, just like her mom. Aren't you, Zoey girl?" I run my finger down the slope of her cheek, in a constant state of awe when I'm around Amelie. Add our daughter to the mix, and it's a whole different scenario.

We're so lost in our own little world that when the nurse asks for us to take Zoey to check her vitals and measurements, I'm annoyed. In the book that Amelie hates, they prepare you for this; it doesn't mean I like it.

"We won't be long. A few minutes tops, then we'll come back, and you can try to get her to latch if you're breastfeeding. If not, we'll get the bottles ready for you." I nod. Amelie looks forlorn. I'm ready to tell them they can wait a few minutes longer when Amelie shakes her head.

"Go with her. Do not take your eyes off our daughter, Boston, or I will get out of this bed and kick you in the balls." I love when she gets feisty like this. Amelie doesn't ask for a lot, not material things, not going out to expensive dinners. My money is worthless to her. When she does ask something of me, it's important. Even if I think she's watched one too many documentaries, she's worried they'll somehow take your child when you're not looking, switch it with another baby, and, well, you never know.

"I'm going. I won't leave her side." I kiss her one last time. Even if it kills me to leave Amelie, our daughter needs us more, and Amelie's request isn't unfathomable, especially after the shit we went through months ago.

The nurses are already working on our baby girl as I make my way toward them. They move so I can stand and watch as they clean her up, take her measurements, and swaddle her tightly, the pink bonnet secured. "Here's baby girl Wescott, twenty-one inches long and nine pounds two ounces." Jesus, it's no wonder Amelie struggled with pushing.

"Thank you." They place our bundle of joy in my arms, making sure she's in the crook of my arm and I'm comfortable with her before I hurry back to the mother of my child and light of my life.

Epilogue

AMELIE

ONE YEAR LATER

"I'M NOT SIGNING these damn papers, beautiful." That would be my future husband on the other side of the door right before our ceremony is due to start. Our daughter is currently with my mom, sleeping, blissfully unaware she'll be walking down the aisle, so to speak, in a wagon. I'm sure taking over the entire wedding with the cuteness overload exploding. I don't mind it, not with our Zoey girl. What Boston is bemoaning is the fact that I sought out Sylvester without his knowledge to protect his assets.

"Sign them, or we're not getting married." I take a sip of my champagne and spin on my heel, making sure not to spill any on my wedding dress. I'm pretty sure Nessa and Millie would yell at me should that happen. Besides, it was me who tried on, no lie, nearly twenty-five dresses during three appointments. How I managed to keep them as friends after is still up for debate.

"Are you really not going to tell him?" Nessa asks. I shrug my shoulders. This makes the making up all the better. You see, when you've been with Boston as long as I have, you learn what works and what doesn't. His number one pet peeve is waiting. Patience is not his strong suit; he's used to getting his way, throwing around big terms or throwing money at business matters to close the deal.

"Of course she's not, this is Amelie we're talking about," Eden says, my girl gang is surrounding me and I love them for it.

"Should I?" I ask Millie. Nessa gives in too easily, especially when it comes to Parker. Millicent is more like I am with Boston when it comes to Ezra; the girl can make the man grovel.

"Eh, you've made the man wait over a year to get married. I think you hold the torch on stretching his patience thin. If you're not careful, he'll pick the lock, toss you over his shoulder, and your grand entrance will be ruined." Damn it, she's right. Boston was ready to have our wedding while I was pregnant. There was no freaking way I was going dress shopping or waddling my ass down an aisle while pregnant with Zoey. And after she was born, LeBlanc Inn part deux was ready to open, Four Brothers opened a month before, and we both hit the ground running. Boston more than me, which did not make it easy to stay on solid footing. A newborn, two business entities, it was a harrowing time. Finally, we sat down, set a date that would work around a not so busy season for the Inn, and, well, Four Brothers is doing better than I think Boston even expected.

"Fine, I guess I'm going to ruin the grand reveal. That whole not seeing the bride before the big day isn't something this group of brothers could ever understand." Boston was not having it. I'd booked a room at the Inn, bags were packed, and I was ready to head out the door when he caught wind of what I was up to. Needless to say, he pulled out his secret weapon, tossed me over his shoulder and carried me up the stairs, making me see the error of my ways while sending me into multiple orgasms.

"You won't regret it," Millie says.

"And then we can all get this show on the road, folks," Nessa inputs. I walk toward the door, take one last gulp of the champagne before opening the door.

"Amelie, for the love of God, open the door. The least you can do is discuss this dumb paper you've signed and now are waiting on mine." I fling the door open. Boston Wescott in a tux, holy mother of meatballs is he devastatingly handsome. He always is. I prefer the man shirt-less, holding our baby girl against his chest while wearing a pair of loose cotton shorts as he dances with her in the kitchen, a slow sway of his hips, and when he grabs my waist to include me, yep, it's enough for me to start asking about trying for our second baby. But right now, it's a different look entirely, knowing by the end of the day, we'll officially be man and wife. It's sexy in its own right.

"Sign the papers, Boston, but maybe you should read them first besides the header that states prenuptial agreement?"

"Jesus Christ, Amelie, you are fucking beauti-ful." The papers he was holding in one hand tumble to the floor.

"And you're not too bad on the eyes yourself." I bend down to pick up the papers. "Boston, this protects both of us. It's not a me against you or you against me scenario. We both have property, money, and you have Four Brothers. Should something ever happen between us, I do not want to come between what you all have successfully built," I tell him, holding the papers out.

"I still don't like it, but if it gets you to the damn altar, I'll sign the damn papers, beautiful. You've got more than any money I could ever make.

I've got you, and you've got me." This time, it's me who lets the papers flutter to the ground. Makeup be damned. I need his lips on mine and Boston's arms wrapped around me. He understands me entirely. His tongue flicks at my upper lip. A sigh leaves me, and Boston slides inside, tongue tangling with mine, both of his hands cupping my upper back, bringing me closer. I'm grateful I didn't pick a ball gown dress and instead found an off-the-shoulder sweetheart neckline, beige with floral embroidery fitted at the top, flaring at the knees with a slit to help with walking.

"Okay, you two lovebirds, Isabelle called and said move it or lose it, literally. The preacher is ready to leave and not marry you," Nessa states.

"I'll sign the papers later." I roll my eyes, knowing the likelihood of that happening is nil. I let it go. Boston's hand is entwined with mine, and he's leading me to the altar, where I'm finally going to become his wife.

Want more Billionaire Playboys? Playing His Games, Sly and Fawn's book is coming May 7th!

Psst...Theo's is book Five, he'd never let me forget him.

Playing His Games

Amazon

Prologue

Sly

Months Earlier

"Come in," I tell the closed door of my office, the thick heavy door was a welcome edition recently, needing the quiet from the busy hallway. Employees coming and going, the rare appointments I do take, they're outside my walls as well, making it inconducive to talking on the phone with all of the chatter. My current secretary is retiring, the woman is older than me by nearly twenty years, can run circles right along with me and is the only person who can boss me around that isn't family blood related or not. Leslie is a damn fine woman, dealing with the shit she does at Sterling and Associates, we're losing one fuck of a rockstar, putting up with me is hard on a good day. Bitterly aware of my workaholic ways, singular focused when I'm on and off the clock. Hell, I've got a divorce to prove how much I love my job, winning a high profile case gives me more than money, it gives me a God damn boner.

Which is more than my ex-wife did, don't get me wrong, she's not completely at fault, being saddled with someone like myself is not for the weak minded. Leslie and I went into our marriage for a mutual benefit, once two people that would scratch an itch, to married in order for me to make partner at my last practice, her for the money and prestige that came along with my last name. Three years later she hated me, I was bitter towards her, neither one of us in love with each other, the sex had long since dried up as well as the attention Leslie needed and deserved. Our marriage wasn't worth salvaging, while she enjoyed the benefit of being Mrs. Sterling and the money it came with, Leslie wanted more, more attention, more of a husband that I wasn't willing to give her, and she wanted the next big dick with more zeros in his bank account than I did at the time. I wasn't innocent in our relationship, it's why when I came home with divorce papers, giving her a healthy settlement, a quick divorce, she took it and ran. My friend, Shane Peterson, the one who's become a traitorous prick with his recent phone call. I hadn't heard from him in years, each of us working in a different area, him as an influential family attorney, me more in the corporate arena. That didn't stop him from calling in a favor, one that I owed him since he wrote an iron-clad divorce settlement, papers so rock solid Leslie couldn't come crawling back years later crying poor and begging an attorney to take her case and try to squeeze more money out of me. Yeah, I'm a jaded prick, fucking sue me.

Jack Peterson, did his job so well that Leslie made out better than most trophy like house-wives would have, money and a home in upstate New York. Seeing as how she could call bias and now judge could either, the minute the ink dried on our divorce papers, I was formulating a new plan entirely. One that included leaving the law office where I crawled my way up from the bottom of the totem pole to the very top. I'm not ashamed to admit I hated it, hated having a boss, and would much rather work for myself. It was a simple plan that manifested from the ground up which in turn meant I was starting my own firm. It took twelve years to get Sterling and Associates to where it is today, more than one hundred employees, and each one knows my door is an open should they ever need to ask for advice on a case or to talk out a problem.

"Mr. Sterling, Fawn Peterson is here for her first day of training," my secretary, Yolanda opens the door, I glance away from the files I'm currently combing through on my desk, an acquisition in the works for my friends at Four Brothers. When I look up she's not at all who I was expecting, a temptation, forbidden, and I've only gotten a glimpse at the brunette beauty. Jack, her father and assholes of all assholes is an average man, his daughter on the other hand is not. I stand up from my place behind my desk, chair backing up as I do, buttoning my jacket, a damn good thing too. One damn look, and wouldn't you know it, my cock decides it's time to make his presence known. Never mind the fact that I jerked off this morning, attempting to tame the beast, while allowing the anger at myself for going too long between finding relief in a different sort of way. My schedule making it nearly impossible for even an hour of downtime.

"Hello, nice to meet you Fawn Peterson," I step around my desk, a short few steps later, my hand is out to shake hers, eyes unable to stop from taking in the innocent beauty before me, soft light brown hair, hanging loosely well past her shoulders, the ends hitting at Fawn's tits, the silk blouse doing nothing to hide her distended nipples. The thoughts in my head run away, a vision of her amber colored eyes, hooded in pleasure, hair falling down, as she bounces up and down on my cock, seeing the smattering of freckles along the bridge of her nose, dusting across her cheekbones, full lips, that would look and feel lush as hell as they wrapped around my thick length.

"It's a pleasure to meet you, Mr. Sterling," Fawn says, wanting to retort the pleasure is all mine. I don't, talk about inappropriate, her soft hand is incased with my much larger one, unable to keep the smirk off my face, Fawn's eyes are cast downward, fucking hell, a natural submissive nature, my cock grew times harder. Yolanda clears her throat, Fawn drops my hand like it burns her to the touch. As for myself, I'm fucked, well and truly, my new secretary is the epitome of forbidden fruit. She's fifteen years younger than me, a colleagues daughter, and the entire time throughout this five minute interaction, I've been imagining her bent over my desk, taking her against my office door, or her bouncing on my cock, tits ripe and ready for my mouth. And I know without a shadow of a doubt, keeping my hands off the young pretty Fawn Peterson is going to take an act of God.

Amazon

About the Author

Tory Baker is a mom and dog mom, living on the coast of sunny Florida where she enjoys the sun, sand, and water anytime she can. Most of the time you can find her outside with her laptop, soaking up the rays while writing about Alpha men, sassy heroines, and always with a guaranteed happily ever after.

Sign up to receive her **Newsletter** for all the latest news!

Tory Baker's Readers is where you see and hear all of the news first!

Also by Tory Baker

Men in Charge

Make Her Mine

Staking His Claim

Secret Obsession

Billionaire Playboys

Playing Dirty

Playing with Fire

Playing With Her

Playing His Games

Vegas After Dark Series

All Night Long

Late Night Caller

One More Night

About Last Night

One Night Stand

Hart of Stone Family

Tease Me

Hold Me

Kiss Me

Please Me

Touch Me

Feel Me

Diamondback MC Second Gen.

Obsessive

Seductive

Addictive

Protective

Deceptive

Diamondback MC

Dirty

Wild

Bare

Wet

Filthy

Sinful

Wicked

Thick

Bad Boys of Texas

Harder

Bigger

Deeper

Hotter

Faster

Hot Shot Series

Fox

Cruz

Jax

Saint

A Love Like Ours

A Love To Cherish

A Love That Lasts

Stand Alone Titles

Nailed

Going All In

What He Wants

Accidental Daddy

Love Me Forever

Gettin' Lucky

It's Her Love

Meant To Be

Breaking His Rules

Can't Walk Away

Carried Away

In Love With My Best Friend

Must Be Love

Sweet As Candy

Falling For Her

All Yours

Sweet Nothings Book 3—Tory Baker

Loving The Mountain Man

Crazy For You

Trick— The Kelly Brothers

Friend Zoned

His Snow Angel

223 True Love Ln.

Hard Ride

Slow Grind

1102 Sugar Rd.

The Christmas Virgin

Taking Control

Unwrapping His Present

Acknowledgments

Thank you for being here, reading, not just my books but any Author's stories. We do appreciate you more than you know, the reason why we can live out our dream is for readers, bloggers, book-stagrammers, bookmakers, Authors, and everyone in between. THANK YOU!

To my kids: A & A without you I'd be a shell of myself. You helped me find myself in a moment of darkness. Thank you for picking up the slack around the house while I was knee deep in this deadline, cooking, cleaning, and taking care of Remi (our big lug of a Weimaraner). I love you to infinity times infinity.

Amie: Seriously, we don't see each other near enough. Miss you tons!

Jordan: Oh my lanta, the hand holding, the me calling you hysterically crying or laughing, day or night, good or bad. I love you bigger than outer space. If it weren't for you pushing me to write, to see the potential in me, I wouldn't be here.

Mayra: My sprinting partner extraordinaire. Girlfriend, we made it through 2022 ahead of schedule. One day I will fly my butt to California to hug you!

Julia: How do you deal with me and my extra sprinkling of commas? The real MVP, the one who deals with my scatterbrained self, missing deadlines, rescheduling like crazy, and the person I live vicariously through social media.

All this to say, I am and will always be forever grateful, love you all!

Made in United States
Orlando, FL
08 June 2025

61934454R20125